This

A MOST SHOCKING REVELATION!
by Kristi Gold

Living in Sheriff Gavin O'Neal's house is
torture for Valerie Raines. She's determined
to keep her secret mission from him, and he's
determined to seduce her! His advances are so
tempting, she can't resist. And once she's in his
bed, she has to work harder to not reveal
herself over a little pillow talk.

SILHOUETTE DESIRE

IS PROUD TO PRESENT

the conclusion of

A new drama unfolds for six of the state's
wealthiest bachelors.

* * *

Dear Reader,

Celebrate the conclusion of 2005 with the six fabulous novels available this month from Silhouette Desire. You won't be able to put down the scintillating finale to DYNASTIES: THE ASHTONS once you start reading Barbara McCauley's *Name Your Price*. He believes she was bought off by his father...she can't fathom his lack of trust. Neither can deny the passion still pulsing between them.

We are so excited to have Caroline Cross back writing for Desire...and with a brand-new miniseries, MEN OF STEELE. In *Trust Me*, reunited lovers have more to deal with than just relationship troubles—they are running for their lives. Kristi Gold kicks one out of the corral as she wraps up TEXAS CATTLEMAN'S CLUB: THE SECRET DIARY with her story of secrets and scandals, *A Most Shocking Revelation*.

Enjoy the holiday cheer found in Joan Elliott Pickart's *A Bride by Christmas*, the story of a wedding planner who believes she's jinxed never to be a bride herself. Anna DePalo is back with another millionaire playboy who finally meets his match, in *Tycoon Takes Revenge*. And finally, welcome brand-new author Jan Colley to the Desire lineup with *Trophy Wives*, a story of lies and seduction not to be missed.

Be sure to come back next month when we launch a new and fantastic twelve-book family dynasty, THE ELLIOTTS.

Melissa Jeglinski

Melissa Jeglinski
Senior Editor
Silhouette Books

Please address questions and book requests to:
Silhouette Reader Service
U.S.: 3010 Walden Ave., P.O. Box 1325, Buffalo, NY 14269
Canadian: P.O. Box 609, Fort Erie, Ont. L2A 5X3

A MOST
Shocking
REVELATION

KRISTI GOLD

Silhouette® Desire

Published by Silhouette Books

America's Publisher of Contemporary Romance

Special thanks and acknowledgment are given
to Kristi Gold for her contribution to the
TEXAS CATTLEMAN'S CLUB:
THE SECRET DIARY series.

 SILHOUETTE BOOKS

ISBN 0-373-76695-5

A MOST SHOCKING REVELATION

Copyright © 2005 by Harlequin Books S.A.

Visit Silhouette Books at www.eHarlequin.com

Printed in U.S.A.

Books by Kristi Gold

Silhouette Desire

Cowboy for Keeps #1308
Doctor for Keeps #1320
His Sheltering Arms #1350
Her Ardent Sheikh #1358
*Dr. Dangerous #1415
*Dr. Desirable #1421
*Dr. Destiny #1427
His E-Mail Order Wife #1454
The Sheikh's Bidding #1485
*Renegade Millionaire #1497
Marooned with a Millionaire #1517
Expecting the Sheikh's Baby #1531
Fit for a Sheikh #1576
Challenged by the Sheikh #1586

†*Persuading the Playboy King* #1600
†*Unmasking the Maverick Prince* #1606
†*Daring the Dynamic Sheikh* #1612
Mistaken for a Mistress #1669
A Most Shocking Revelation #1695

*Marrying an M.D.
†The Royal Wager

KRISTI GOLD

has always believed that love has remarkable healing powers and feels very fortunate to be able to weave stories of romance and commitment. Since her first Desire novel debuted in 2000, she's sold over twenty books to date. A classic seat-of-the pants writer, she attributes her ability to write fast to a burning need to see how the book ends.

As a bestselling author, National Readers' Choice winner and Romance Writers of America RITA® Award finalist, she's learned that although accolades are wonderful, the most cherished rewards come from personal stories shared by readers, and networking with other authors, both published and aspiring.

You can reach Kristi through her Web site at www.kristigold.com or through snail mail at P.O. Box 9070, Waco, Texas 76714 (Please include a SASE for a response).

To fellow Cattleman's Club authors
Cindy Gerard, Shirley Rogers, Brenda Jackson,
Michelle Celmer and Sara Orwig for your assistance
in developing this series. Many thanks, ladies.
It's been a pleasure working with you!

Prologue

From the diary of Jessamine Golden
December 5, 1910

Dear Diary,
Today is the day I will confront Edgar Halifax. Now that I have his stolen gold, I will do whatever it takes to end his reign of terror. Not only did he murder my father but he also murdered Nicholas Devlin and laid the blame on Richard Windcroft. Edgar now has the blood of two innocent men on his hands and who knows how many others. Though he will try to kill me, I vow to fight for my life, even if I, too, must commit murder.

If I survive, I will leave Royal behind, the only home I have ever known. I will go far away from this place known as an outlaw. I will also leave Sheriff Brad Webster behind, the only man I have ever loved. The man who plans to arrest me tonight.

I am leaving a map that will point the way to the buried gold, but should it fall into enemy hands, the exact hiding place can be found only by whoever possesses my special heart pendant etched with roses—the one given to me by my true love.

I will also leave this diary behind in hopes that one day the truth will finally be known.

One

December 2005

Sheriff Gavin O'Neal hated being jarred from a deep sleep—unless a woman happened to be doing the jarring. Unfortunately tonight that was not the case, and it hadn't been for quite a while.

With an unsolved murder hanging over his head and enough mayhem in Royal, Texas, to drive a weaker man to drink, his so-cial—and sex—life had been nonexistent for months. Probably just as well. Another complication was the last thing he needed right now. He also didn't need a 1:00 a.m. domestic-disturbance call at a pig farm after a tough week at work, but that's exactly what he faced at the moment. With several of his deputies out of commission because of a raging flu epidemic, he'd had no choice but to answer the dispatcher's summons himself.

As he navigated the winding rural road, Gavin flipped the heat on high and the radio on low, muttering a string of curses aimed at the conditions and the call. Whatever had warranted this late-night expedition to Harvey Joe Raleigh's house, it had better be good. The guy had a used-car-salesman swagger and a big mouth, and Gavin didn't like him one bit. He liked him even less now.

Gavin turned up the pothole-filled drive that led to the rickety white farmhouse and skirted a graveyard of beat-up cars and run-down livestock pens. He pulled up beside a rusty truck, braked hard and yanked the SUV into park. The overpowering smell of hogs greeted him as he trudged up the dirt path toward the house. If that didn't wake him up, nothing would. The weathered porch, decorated with a string of helter-skelter holiday lights draped from the eaves overhead, groaned beneath his weight as he scaled the three steps to the entry. Considering his recent luck, he could end up falling through the dried-out boards and breaking something vital.

Before he could knock on the door, fifty-something Sue Raleigh appeared wearing a tattered blue terry housecoat and an apologetic look. "I'm sorry for getting you out so late, Sheriff."

Gavin had liked Sue immediately when he'd met her a few months before, although he questioned how such a nice, proper lady could have ended up with a worthless moron like Harvey Joe. "No problem. What's going on?"

She leaned out the screen and pointed to her left. "It's our renter. She lives in the little house out back. According to Harvey Joe, she threatened him."

A woman? She had to be tough to endure living in this place. "Is she armed?"

Sue shook her head. "I don't know. Harvey went to take care of it."

Talk about walking in with limited information. "So you don't know if she's armed or if Harvey's in any real trouble?"

"I'm not sure. He told me to stay here and call you."

"What's the renter's name?"

"Valerie Raines."

Valerie Raines? "You mean the waitress down at the Royal Diner?" *Brilliant, O'Neal.* In a town the size of Royal, how many Valerie Raineses would there be?

"Yes, that's the one," Sue said.

Gavin had a hard time believing any of this. "She doesn't seem like the violent type."

"I didn't think so either, but people aren't always what they seem."

He couldn't agree more, a hard lesson learned in his line of work. "Okay. I'll see what I can do."

As he strode through the damp grass toward the ramshackle cottage, Gavin tugged his collar up as protection against the north wind and wondered what he was about to encounter. Granted, he didn't mind seeing Val again, even under these circumstances. She was as cute as a blue heeler pup, and he doubted she'd turned pit bull overnight. Knowing Harvey Joe, he'd probably done something to warrant Val's rant. Not to mention, she was a slip of a woman half Harvey's size. Gavin couldn't imagine her doing the guy any real harm.

He arrived at the house to find the door ajar, but even if it had been closed and made of steel, half the county could probably hear the sound of the feminine voice shouting, "I mean it, you jerk! Stay right where you are."

Gavin stepped inside the cracker-box living room to find Harvey backed against the wall, Val standing before him, wielding a mop. The sight was pretty comical at that—one balding, beer-bellied farmer looking bug-eyed and one wisp of a waitress looking downright furious. She also looked mighty sweet wearing that oversize white shirt, baggy pajama bottoms and her blond hair piled high atop her head.

"What's going on here?" Gavin asked, trying to keep his tone light.

"Now you're in trouble," Harvey said while pointing a stubby finger at Valerie. "She's crazy, Sheriff. I want her arrested."

Val turned her face toward Gavin and eyed him with surprise that melted into frustration. "Oh, great. I should have known he'd call you. But that's okay because he's the one who should be arrested." She emphasized her words by waving the mop at Harvey's groin.

Gavin took a step closer. "What seems to be the problem exactly?"

"I told you, Sheriff, she's nuts," Harvey said.

She pointed the mop at Harvey's face. "I'm not nuts. I have about two inches of water in the bathroom from a leaky pipe beneath the sink, no heat and rats as big as small terriers in the kitchen. I've asked him nicely to fix the problems, but he won't listen. When I bent over to show him the pipe, he grabbed my butt and I got tired of being nice."

Gavin gritted his teeth and spoke through them. "That true, Harvey?"

The man looked only slightly chagrined. "I didn't grab nothin'. I just brushed up against her."

"Liar," Valerie snapped.

"And as far as the other stuff goes," Harvey continued, "she ain't payin' all that much to live here."

"All that much?" She jabbed the mop in Harvey's chest. "If you charged me a dollar, it would be too much."

Time to take some action, Gavin decided. If he didn't, Val could very well turn that mop around and beat Harvey over the head with the stick handle instead of the strings. "Drop the mop, Val, and step away from Harvey Joe," he said, rather pleased that he'd maintained a straight face while delivering the order.

Val lifted her chin and didn't move. "Not until he promises me he'll call a heating repairman, a plumber and an exterminator tonight."

"I ain't callin' no one tonight," Harvey said. "I'm not gonna pay overtime rates. You can light the stove for heat and use the old outhouse out back."

"You idiot!" When Val raised the mop, Gavin was on her fast, wresting the thing from her grip and grabbing her around the middle.

Like the coward he was, Harvey Joe dashed out the door, letting go a few foul words aimed at the woman in Gavin's arms.

"Let me go!" Val shouted, and it took all Gavin's power to keep her from wriggling out of his grasp. For such a little thing, the lady was pretty strong. And she smelled good, too. She was certainly doing some potent things to him with her bottom pressed against his fly. The tighter he held her, the more she struggled against him and the more he weakened. He had an atomic blonde in his arms bent on destroying his dignity, but she didn't even realize it. Yet.

He brought his mouth to her ear and said, "Val, if you don't be still, I'm going to charge you with torturing a peace officer."

She stopped struggling and looked back at him. "Torturing *you?*"

"Yeah. If you think that's my gun at your backside, you're wrong. I'm wearing a shoulder holster."

Both awareness and a deep blush passed over her pretty face. "Maybe you should let me go then."

On one hand, that was a wise idea. On the other, he didn't exactly mind her brand of torture. But this was business, and that meant defusing the situation immediately. "Are you going to take off and go after Harvey Joe?"

She sighed. "No."

Gavin loosened his hold on her, then took her by the shoulders and turned her around to face him. "Okay, let's talk about your options."

"What options?"

He took a quick look around and he didn't like what he saw. The place was disgusting, from the tattered furniture to the dingy tile floor. It didn't smell much better than the pigsty outside. "This house isn't fit for decent living, so it would be best if you find somewhere else to stay."

"I can't afford a hotel—or at least any I care to stay at."

That gave Gavin an idea. A good idea. He'd had a thing for Valerie Raines for months now, and she'd responded to his overtures with a few sassy jabs with her straight-razor tongue, unfortunately only in the figurative sense. If he had her in his house, had her undivided attention, even if only temporarily, then maybe he could convince her that he wasn't just looking for a good time. Truth was, he liked her. A lot. "You can stay with me for the night…or as long as you need."

Her eyes went wide. Deep blue eyes that had gotten Gavin's attention on more than one occasion at the diner. "Are you insane?"

Not yet, but he was getting there fast. "I have a guest room. A couple, in fact."

She shook her head and folded her arms beneath her breasts. "I can always sleep in the city park, thank you very much."

"Okay. Suit yourself."

She eyed the handcuffs he withdrew from his jacket pocket. "What are you doing?"

"I'm going to give you another option—the county jail."

Her gaze snapped from the cuffs to his face, and he saw a flash of fear in her eyes. "You're going to arrest me?"

"Yep, unless you get this fool notion out of your head that you'd be better off on the streets. We've got a killer on the loose and you could be his next victim. The only way I know you'll be safe is with me or in a cell. Take your pick."

He saw several emotions cross her face, starting with fury then finally resignation. "All right. I'll go home with you." She pointed at him. "But only for tonight."

Gavin couldn't deny the sense of satisfaction. "Now that we've settled your arrangements," he told her, "go pack a bag."

She tugged at her shirt and started down the narrow hallway. "Fine. I'll be back in a minute."

"I'll go with you."

He took all of two steps before she spun around. "That's not necessary."

"Yeah, it is. I don't want you going out a window."

She gave him a serious scowl. "Does this mean I'm your prisoner, Sheriff?"

"No, but I am responsible for you tonight, Val, so get used to it."

That earned him a sour look. "For the hundredth time, it's Valerie. And I'm responsible for myself."

She was definitely going to be trouble. "Let me rephrase that. Tonight I'm responsible for your *safety*. But again, the jail's an option if you'd rather go that route."

Her shoulders slumped from surrender. "Okay. Message received."

Val started back down the hallway and turned right into a bedroom, Gavin close on her heels. He stopped at the door and leaned a shoulder against the facing to watch her retrieve a bag from under the rickety bed and a few clothes from the dresser. When she came to the drawer housing her underclothes, she shot him a dirty look, but that didn't cause him to avert his gaze, although he probably should have. Viewing her underwear wasn't necessarily a good idea, especially when she systematically held each pair up for inspection before placing it in the bag. No doubt about it, she was taunting him, and his body was taking the bait. He shifted against the subtle stirring where her bottom had been only moments before, cautioning himself to behave.

Valerie closed the drawer, then took a small wooden chest from the top of the dresser, cuddling it close to her breasts, as though she was afraid that it might grow legs and run away. "Special keepsakes?" he asked.

She laid the chest on top of the clothes and zipped the bag. "Yes. If I leave it, Harvey might take it upon himself to pawn what little jewelry I have left."

Gavin couldn't argue with that. "Are you ready now?"

"Almost." After she slipped the bag and her purse strap over her shoulder, she walked to the closet and retrieved the pink polyester uniform dresses she always wore at work. On most women, they wouldn't be considered flattering—old-fashioned, like the Royal Diner. But as far as Gavin was concerned, Val looked good in them. Hell, she'd look good in a burlap sack. She'd look even better in nothing at all.

She turned and announced, "Okay, now I'm ready."

Unfortunately so was Gavin. A little too ready to be considered a gentleman. He pushed off the doorjamb and gestured toward the hall. "After you."

She breezed past him in a rush and it was all he could do to keep up with her without sprinting. At the front door she told him, "I put my car in the shop today, which means you'll have to drive us."

He'd planned to do that anyway. Her mechanical problems had fortunately saved him from another argument. "How did you plan to get to work tomorrow?"

"Sue volunteered to drop me off, and since that's no longer an option, looks like you'll have that responsibility, too."

He winked. "Not a problem at all. I like to eat breakfast at the diner anyway."

He opened the screen and she stormed out before he could even get the door closed behind him. She was strong and she was fast and she was definitely piquing Gavin's curiosity, among other things.

For the past six months she'd remained a mystery to most of the town, including Gavin. But he liked mysteries and he wanted to solve this one named Valerie Raines. After all, that's what he did. And he did it well.

Valerie Raines had secrets she refused to reveal to anyone, especially Gavin O'Neal. She did not intend to get too friendly with him. She did not intend to spend more than one night in his house. And she certainly didn't intend to keep staring at him, yet she couldn't seem to help herself.

Not exactly staring, but she did risk a few glances his way while he peered out the windshield, silently navigating the rural roads, one large hand resting on his thigh, the other braced on the steering wheel. He had a strong profile to match his strong personality. His jaw was square and his neatly-trimmed hair was the color of warm earth. The small cleft in his chin had held her fascination on more than one occasion, and so had his eyes. Brown eyes that seemed to change depending on his mood—lighter when he was being mischievous, much darker when he sported a serious expression, which wasn't all that often. A beautiful man with an abundance of charm. A man she should avoid like the flu plaguing the town.

Unbeknownst to the sheriff, something about him had resonated in Valerie from the first time she'd met him. Maybe it was his honor or his easy smile. Whatever the case might be, she'd always secretly reacted with excitement every time he'd stepped foot in the diner, disrupting her carefully crafted composure. But even though she'd tried to avoid him, had tried to ignore his flirtations, for the past few weeks he'd begun to splinter her resistance. Entering his private world, if only for one night, could play havoc with her defenses, the way his close proximity at the moment was playing havoc with her heartbeat.

"What's wrong with your car?" he asked, intruding into Valerie's thoughts.

The car was too old, and she was too broke to buy another one. "Transmission leak. I tried to see if I could repair it, but I wasn't successful."

"You tried to fix it?"

Valerie glanced at him long enough to notice he looked as shocked as he'd sounded. "Yes, I tried to fix it, heavy emphasis on *tried*. I know how to change a tire and the oil and replace a battery. I can do a few other minor repairs, too. But without the car on a rack, it was too hard to tell what was happening with it."

"You're pretty amazing."

That brought her gaze back to him. "Why? Because I'm a woman and I know a thing or two about mechanics?"

"Yeah. I'm just kind of surprised."

He definitely would be surprised if he knew everything about her. "The more you know, the more money you can save in the long run."

"Who has your car now?" he asked.

"Rhodes Garage downtown."

"Bill Rhodes is good, and honest."

And expensive, especially when it came to major repairs, or so Valerie had heard. Her funds were already limited, and she had to rely solely on her salary now instead of her savings. But the bills she'd incurred for her grandmother's hospital stay had been all but paid off, the only real positive accomplishment in recent months.

"Are you warm enough, Val?" Gavin asked.

Oh, she was warm all right. Hot, as a matter of fact, for several reasons, the least of which was her inability to ignore his charisma. She also didn't care for anyone shortening her name. Only one person had been allowed to do so, and now her beloved grandmother was gone. "As I've said before, it's Valerie, not Val. And I'm fine."

"You don't sound fine."

She sent another glance at Gavin and cursed all the things that made him too attractive to overlook. But ignore him she would. Or at least she would try. "Okay, I'm as fine as someone who's being held captive can be."

"I'm not holding you captive. I'm giving you a helping hand. You should appreciate it. When I told Harvey Joe I wasn't arresting you, he wasn't happy about it."

Another positive, both the lack of arrest and ticking Harvey Joe off. She shifted as close to the door as the seat belt allowed. "And exactly how did you get around not arresting me, since he probably had a legitimate complaint?"

He took his hand from his thigh long enough to scrub a palm over his shadowed jaw. "I told him that I'd tell his wife he was trying a little slap and tickle out on their renter and that I'd encourage you to file attempted sexual assault charges."

Valerie had to admit she appreciated his assistance. "What happened tonight, that wasn't like me. I'm not a violent person."

His laugh was low and compelling. "I tend to believe that. I don't consider a string mop as a hardened criminal's weapon of choice."

Valerie couldn't stop her own laugh. A small one, but still a laugh. "I guess not. I just happened to have it in my hand when he grabbed me. I lost my temper."

"Harvey Joe had no right to touch you. You had to defend yourself."

"You don't know the half of it." And he didn't. About Harvey Joe's penchant for lewd remarks or her reasons for being in Royal. Better things stayed that way for now, if not indefinitely.

"We're here," Gavin announced as they took a left turn into a lengthy drive lined with white piped fencing.

Valerie couldn't make out much more than a few lights dotting the horizon as they ascended a slight hill. But as the residence came into view, to say she was surprised by Gavin O'Neal's ranch was a definite understatement. The sprawling stone house looked to be four times the size of her recent residence—and apparently sixty times the luxury. Yet as she followed the sheriff through the heavy front door, that theory proved partially untrue. She'd expected more opulence, but the area was relatively unadorned, the walls all but bare with the exception of a few framed prints of landscapes. She'd expected more country than contemporary, and that, too, was not the case. No animal horns or heads decorating the hearth. No cowhide furniture. Just simple brown suede sofas with matching chairs, plain oak tables, woven rugs in black and russet tones covering beige slate-tiled floors. The stone fireplace spanned upward to the high ceiling, dividing what appeared to be an open loft surrounded by a rough-hewn railing, wooden stairs flanking each end of the room.

She was only mildly aware that the door had closed and totally unaware that Gavin was standing behind her until he said, "Welcome to my home."

Valerie faced him and managed a weak smile. "Thank you. I really do appreciate your hospitality and I'll be out of your hair soon. I'll start looking for a new place in the morning."

He gave her a grin designed to melt an ice cap. "Don't rush off on my account. There's plenty of room here for the both of us."

Valerie didn't necessarily agree with that. Right now he made the massive room seem to shrivel and made her feel equally small—in a nice kind of way. "I'm sure you don't need me hanging around, disrupting your social life."

He looked somewhat amused. "Not much opportunity for a social life in Royal. Most women are either married, engaged or over the age of sixty."

"I suppose that's true." Considering his kindness, she decided to make a concession. "And you may call me Val."

He studied her a long moment, drawing her further into his dark, dark gaze. "I don't want to do anything you don't want me to do."

"Believe me, I'm not inclined to do anything I don't want to do, Sheriff."

"Okay, Val. As long as you call me Gavin. In this house, I'm not the sheriff."

But he was incredibly sexy with his ruffled brown hair and sleepy brown eyes. "It's a deal." She offered her hand and he took it without hesitation. But instead of giving it a shake, he held it in his callused palm for a long moment, his gaze never faltering. And Valerie allowed the gesture for a few moments before reality wormed its way into her haywire psyche. She could not accept anything but his friendship—cautious friendship. If he knew the truth, knew who she was and what she had planned, he could try to thwart her goals. Worse, he might view her as so many had in her lifetime—as someone not worth knowing.

Valerie tugged out of his grasp and released her breath. "We should go to bed now." And that sounded like a proposition.

The sheriff's trademark smile crept back in. "The thought has crossed my mind."

Valerie's, too, and that was one thought she couldn't afford. "Mind showing me to my room?"

Gavin didn't even try to mask his disappointment. "Okay, if I must."

She sent him a wry grin. "Yes, you must."

"Follow me then."

Valerie snatched her bag from the floor and trailed behind him, keeping her gaze centered on his broad back. She refused to give in to the definite flicker of threatening desire or feminine inquisitiveness that dictated she check out the territory below his belt. She'd avoided that very thing when he came into the diner, disregarding his presence until he was seated at a booth. From the beginning she'd had a goal, and fraternizing with Gavin O'Neal hadn't been a part of it. It couldn't be. But just this one time she gave in to her curiosity and let her gaze drift downward. As suspected, he filled out his jeans nicely. Very nicely. Too nicely.

Valerie nearly collided with him when he came to a halt at a closed door, her face almost landing in the middle of his back, saved only by a quick step away from him.

"This is the biggest room, aside from mine," he said as he opened the door. "It has a private bath."

She stepped past him without even a cursory glance in his direction. Instead she focused on the bed, a heavy four-poster draped in a red comforter. The floors were covered in a plush beige carpet, and a lone bureau sat angled in the corner. A small TV rested on a stand across from a narrow lounger on the far side of the room. Closed beige drapes spanned the wall, and Valerie would guess they opened to windows overlooking the surrounding land.

She walked to the bed and ran her hand over one post. "It's going to be nice when my feet hit the floor in the morning without turning into ice blocks."

"It's simple but comfortable."

She finally turned to him. "Simple suits me fine."

He narrowed his gaze. "I suspect there's nothing simple about you."

In a way, he was right, especially when it came to her secrets. "Believe what you will, Sheriff, but I've never required a lot in the way of material objects. To me, this room is the equivalent of a four-star hotel suite."

"Glad you like it." He took a step into the room, shrugged off his jacket and draped it and the holster housing his gun over one arm. "You can hang your things in the closet, and all the drawers are empty."

"Thanks." She put her uniforms away, and even after she began to unpack he continued to watch her. As she had back at the old house, she withdrew her bras and panties from the bag and took her time placing them in the bureau's top drawer, hoping to send him on his way. But he didn't budge.

He did say, "I didn't know you were living at a hog farm."

With a prime pig, no less. "I've only been there a couple of weeks."

"Where were you staying before that?"

"The Skyline Motor Inn." She flashed him a quick smile. "Have an hour, we've got a room waiting. No charge for the roaches."

"That's a seedy place."

She concentrated on settling several pairs of her jeans into the next drawer. "Yes, which is why I left. I didn't feel too safe."

"How did you end up in Royal?"

She rearranged clothes that didn't need rearranging to avoid his gaze, but she couldn't really avoid the question without rousing suspicion. "I answered the ad Manny put in the paper."

"Where did you live before you came here?"

"Several places." The first lie. She'd only lived in one place before she'd settled in Royal, another fact that would remain hidden from him for the time being.

"Have you always been a waitress?"

Valerie shut the drawer and leaned back against the bureau. "Aren't you tired yet?" She hid a fake yawn behind her hand.

He smiled. "Not really, but you are."

She stretched her arms above her head. "Yes, I am. I need to be up early in the morning."

"Me, too." He released the top button on his starched beige shirt. "Just tell me what time and I'll wake you up."

She was having one heck of a time thinking since he seemed bent on removing his shirt. "Very early." She pointed at the bedside clock radio. "I'll set the alarm so you don't have to bother."

He slipped another button. "I don't mind waking you."

Valerie minded that he kept undressing. It made her uncomfortable, and not in a bad way. "I'll get myself up."

He set his gun and jacket on the bureau and tugged the shirt-tails from his jeans before tackling the remaining buttons. "Suit yourself then. Anything else you need?"

Yeah. She needed him to leave his clothes completely intact and her alone with her devious thoughts. "Not that I can think of."

When he started toward her, Valerie's breath hitched hard in her chest. But he kept going without giving her a glance.

"What are you doing now?" she asked as he pulled the curtain aside.

"Making sure the windows are locked tight."

Good grief. "I promise I'm not going to climb out, if that's what's worrying you."

He settled the curtain back into place and turned, his shirt now gaping to reveal a monumental muscled chest covered in a fine mat of golden-brown hair. "I'm making sure no one gets in."

"Are you trying to scare me?" He certainly was shaking her up.

"Just making sure you're safe."

Valerie didn't feel all that safe at the moment. She felt a little too warm and way too distracted. "Thanks."

"Guess I'll go to bed now," he said. But he just stood there, tempting her with his sex appeal and sultry smile.

"Do you remember where your bed is?" she asked when he didn't move.

He pointed to his right. "Next door. Just a few steps away if you need anything from me."

Valerie noted the invitation in his eyes and disregarded the strong urge to answer it. "I'm sure I have everything I need."

"Okay then." When he passed her again, he patted her cheek. "Sleep tight, Val."

She'd be lucky if she slept at all. "You, too, Gavin. And thanks again."

He paused at the door and sent her another sexy smile. "You're welcome. Remember, if you need anything from me, all you have to do is ask. Better still, just whistle."

"You mean like this?" Valerie placed her pinkies in her mouth and let go an ear-piercing shrill.

Gavin grinned. "Yeah, that'll work. Or maybe something a little quieter so you don't wake up all the coyotes in the county. See you in the morning."

After he headed out the door, Valerie just couldn't help herself. She whistled again, sending him back into the room. "You called?"

She laughed. "Just checking."

His smile collapsed into a frown. "You remember that story about the boy who cried wolf, don't you?"

"Sorry," she said, although she really wasn't. At least she

could get another good look at him. "I won't do it again unless I really need something from you."

He gripped the door, his expression turning seriously seductive. "And one of these days I just might make you whistle."

Finally he left, closing the door behind him. Valerie dropped onto the edge of the mattress and covered her face with both hands. Truth was, sleep didn't seem all that appealing at the moment. Knowing Gavin O'Neal much better did. And that was too dangerous to consider.

Pushing off the bed, Valerie walked to the bureau, opened the keepsake box and pulled out the reminder of why she couldn't focus on Gavin O'Neal. For the hundredth time she read the letter left to her by her grandmother. The letter that had prompted Valerie's visit to Royal to search for her past in order to move forward with her future.

My dearest Val,
This envelope came to me a few years before, sent by a law firm that had been instructed to hold it until the appropriate time, per your great-great-grandmother's instructions. I am too old to take on this task, so I will leave it up to you.

You are a wonderful, remarkable woman, Valerie, so full of goodness and compassion. I failed your mother in many ways, but I would like to think that I made up for my mistakes with you. Always remember, you are nothing like her. You deserve the best, and I hope that you will find happiness after so much hardship. Perhaps this will help.
All my love,
Gran

After putting the letter away, Valerie pulled out the journal from beneath the other clues that should help her accomplish her mission. Every evening before she retired she wrote down the details of her day, a habit she'd formed at an early age. Sometimes that habit had been the only thing that had gotten her through the toughest of times, through the pain. She dug a pen from her purse, took a seat on the lounger and opened her book of memories, the newest volume among many others she'd kept over the years, and began to write.

I'm in Gavin O'Neal's house after a ridiculous run-in with Mr. Raleigh, the swine. I shouldn't be here. I shouldn't be thinking what I'm thinking about the sheriff—that he leaves me weak-kneed and feeling entirely too feminine. He's arrogant. Gorgeous. Too charming for my own good. He had that look in his eyes tonight, that gleam that I've witnessed several times in the diner. The one that says he wants me. But I doubt he would want me if he knew the truth. If he knew about my past transgressions. If he knew my shame. If he knew I'm the great-great-granddaughter of Royal's most infamous and hated outlaw.

For that reason I have to get out of here fast, before I might be tempted to stay.

Two

The following morning Gavin awoke to the smell of coffee wafting into the bedroom. He automatically went for his gun on the nightstand before he realized his stupidity. He seriously doubted he'd been visited by a band of fugitive chefs who'd made themselves at home before planning his demise. As the haze of sleep cleared, he remembered who was in his kitchen—the lady who'd come to his house last night but not to his bed. Unfortunately.

After laying the weapon aside, Gavin sat up and streaked both hands over his face before checking the bedside clock. Five o'clock. Valerie hadn't been kidding when she'd said she was an early riser. But then, so was he, especially at the moment.

He tossed back the covers and draped his legs over the edge of the bed. For a second he considered joining her just as he was—wearing nothing except some serious evidence of his usual morning state of arousal—but that might send her flying out the door and out of his life for good. Instead he stood, tugged on his jeans and headed down the hall on bare feet and without a shirt.

His mother would have claimed he was being ungentlemanly had she still been around to scold him.

The closer he got to the kitchen, the more the excitement began to build. Last night he'd told Valerie only a partial truth—plenty of willing women still existed in Royal if a man knew where to look. And he did. He'd encountered a few in Midland, too, at a conference right after he'd been elected sheriff seven months ago. That was the last time he'd indulged in a woman's company. That was the last time he'd cared to look beyond Valerie Raines and he didn't understand that one bit. Maybe it was the challenge, the chase. Or the fact that she hadn't acted as though she cared for him much since that first time he'd seen her at the diner.

He still planned to get to know her better. He'd seen some serious awareness in her eyes last night when he'd inadvertently begun disrobing in front of her before he'd realized what he was doing. That hadn't stopped him. After her little double lingerie displays, she'd deserved to be caught off guard.

And off guard was exactly how Val looked when Gavin walked into the kitchen to find her at the stove. She'd already dressed in her standard uniform with her hair pulled up in a ponytail. Just once he'd like to see her hair down. He'd really like to see it flowing across his bare chest or belly. Maybe if he'd stuck around a little longer last night he might have had that opportunity. And if he really believed that, then he definitely needed more rest.

Gavin walked up behind Val and peered over her shoulder. "Smells great." And so did she, like some kind of flowers he couldn't quite peg. "You didn't have to go to all this trouble."

"It wasn't any trouble." She briefly regarded him over one shoulder. "Scrambled eggs and sausage links, your favorite."

"How did you know?"

She sent him a frown. "Because you order it at the diner almost every morning."

"True, when I don't have Manny's pancakes."

She gestured toward the dinette with the spatula. "Have a seat. It's ready."

Gavin was more than ready to kiss her. He had been for a while now. He could wait a little longer, when she wasn't cooking. Otherwise, she might whack him with the egg turner, or worse, take the frying pan to his skull. That was a hell of a lot heavier than a mop.

He poured a cup of coffee, black, reluctantly took his usual seat and waited for her to serve him. She was in his house and playing waitress. He didn't really like that at all. "I don't expect you to do this every morning." And that sounded as if he expected her to stay indefinitely. Not a bad idea at that.

She disagreed, apparent when she said, "I don't plan to be here much longer."

Gavin sat back and laced his hands behind his neck. "Sometimes plans go awry."

He almost laughed when she jumped as the toast popped up. No doubt, she was nervous about something.

She filled his plate, turned and approached him with a small smile. "Here you go, Sheriff. The usual."

He straightened and accepted the fork she offered. "What do I owe you?"

"You've already paid me by providing me with a place to land for a bit."

He started to tell her he would have preferred she land in his arms. "Not a problem. You're welcome to stay as long as you'd like."

She took the chair across from him, rested her bent elbow on the table and supported her cheek with her palm. "I'll be leaving as soon as I find a place to stay."

"A decent place to say," he added between bites. "And that might be tough with Christmas only a few weeks away. People don't usually move during the holidays."

She sighed. "You're right about that. I might have to go back to the no-tell motel until after the first of the year."

"No way are you going back there. You're better off here with me."

The look she sent him said she had her reservations about that. "What will the good people of Royal think if they learn I'm living here with you?"

"I don't care what they think. I only care about your well-being."

"Why is that, Gavin?"

Having her call him by his name pleased him. A lot. He pushed his plate away and sat back. "Because you're a nice lady, Val. Besides, if you stay for a while, that will give us a chance to get to know each other better."

She took his plate to the sink and kept her back to him. "You might just decide you don't like what you learn."

An odd thing for Val to say—a woman who seemed to have a world of confidence under normal circumstances. Gavin wondered if she'd been treated badly by a man, maybe even had her heart stomped on a time or two. That would certainly explain her wariness. And he had every intention of proving she was a woman worth knowing, starting now.

Pushing back from the table, Gavin rose on his bare feet and walked to the sink to stand behind her. He rested his hand lightly on her waist and leaned close to her ear. "Tell you what, Val. Odds are I'm going to like you real well. I already do. And my gut tells me nothing's going to change that. I guarantee it."

He felt her frame grow rigid and for a fleeting moment he wondered if it was something he'd said. But he suspected it had more to do with his close proximity. Yet she didn't move away from him and she didn't flinch when he kissed her cheek, then on afterthought kissed her sweet-smelling neck.

And she didn't slug him when he patted her bottom and told her, "I'm going to take a shower and then we can leave."

When he turned away, she stopped him by saying, "You might change your mind about me after a while."

He faced Valerie to find her leaning against the sink, wringing a dish towel in her grasp. Striding to her again, he touched her face when he saw the insecurity calling out from her deep blue eyes. "Let me tell you something, Val. I have good instincts about people. And although I don't pretend to know what's going on in that pretty head of yours most of the time, I do know there's not a thing you can say that would change my mind about you. You're definitely someone worth knowing."

He brushed a soft kiss across her lips and then left the kitchen before he was tempted to do more.

You're definitely someone worth knowing...

Gavin's declaration had haunted Valerie all during the early shift at the diner. Now nearing 2:00 p.m., she continued to think about it and the chaste kiss he'd given her that morning. Think about how she wanted to open up to him. How much she wanted his acceptance. How much she wanted things that she shouldn't want.

Pipe dreams, every one.

She wished for more patrons so she could get her mind off Gavin, but the place was slow at the moment, as it usually was on Friday following the lunchtime crush. Of course, when evening arrived, the crowd would be back in full force, and for that reason, she should enjoy the break.

After clearing off the last littered table, Valerie walked behind the counter and leaned through the opening to the kitchen. Manny Reno was seated near the stove, reading the paper and gnawing a toothpick like a beaver. A bodybuilding beaver. His arms were as big as the hams he prepared for Sunday dinner, and his chest looked as though it might escape from his T-shirt at any given moment. The other waitresses claimed that at one time he'd been a flirt—basically harmless yet still a flirt—but that was before he'd bought the diner from the former owner, Hazel, and married Sheila, the one-time head waitress. Now he was successful, totally smitten and a father-to-be. His and Sheila's apparent happiness had only served to remind Valerie how much she wanted that very thing in the future. Maybe not the near future, but eventually. And she wanted it with someone like Gavin O'Neal. Who was she kidding? She wanted it with Gavin O'Neal.

Forcing her mind back on reality, she tapped the counter to get her boss's attention. "I need to take tomorrow off, Manny," she said, then braced for the fallout.

He glanced up before going back to the sports section. "Okay. Take two days."

Although Manny was always fair, that was just too easy considering they were already shorthanded. "Are you feeling okay?"

"I'm feeling great. Sheila can come in and relieve you."

"I thought you were letting your wife be a lady of leisure, at least until the morning sickness wears off."

He grinned without looking up from the paper. "She's pretty much over that now. In fact, she's suffering from what she calls 'raging hormones.' I like raging hormones real well."

Obviously those raging hormones, like the flu, were going around town. Valerie had definitely come down with a strong case of them. "Are you sure she won't mind?"

"Not if it means she can be with me all day." He turned the page without looking up. "And besides, the sheriff called me this morning and told me you needed some time off. When he speaks, people listen."

Valerie tossed the rag aside and later planned to toss a few words at Gavin for his unwelcome interference. "He did, did he?"

"Yeah. He didn't say why, but I figured that was none of my business. I also decided he owed me one, which means he might go easy on me if I get caught speeding when I need to get home to take care of Sheila's hormones."

If he mentioned hormones one more time, Valerie might be tempted to scream. "I have to find a new place to stay, that's why I need the time off."

Manny glanced up again. "What's wrong with your old one?"

"Let's just say Harvey Joe and I didn't see eye to eye on the terms of our rental agreement. I'd prefer not to live with rats, even if they are drowning from major water leaks."

"I told you Harvey Joe's a jerk before you decided to move in there." Manny shook out the paper and stood. "Where are you staying now?"

No need to lie to her boss. Considering Royal's small-town penchant for gossip, word would get out sooner than later. "*Temporarily* with Sheriff O'Neal."

Manny laughed. Loudly. "I knew you two had a thing for each other."

"We don't have a *thing* for each other." Okay, just a minor fabrication. "I'm staying in the guest room, so get your mind out of the sewer, Manny."

He showed her a toothy grin before opening the oven to retrieve his famous coconut pie. "If you say so, Valerie. But I'm thinking he'd rather have you in his bedroom."

Valerie was overcome with the urge to protest, until the bell sounded, indicating a customer. She turned to see the somewhat snooty Gretchen Halifax breeze into the diner and head to the corner booth by the window. She removed her coat to reveal a gray wool suit, perfectly pressed and definitely expensive. The city councilwoman reminded Valerie of a mink, all lithe and too slick. Nothing about her seemed real, from her pale blond hair to her ageless face to her phony facade.

If Valerie had her way, someone else would wait on her. Right now, she was the only waitress available. She took her time strolling to the counter to retrieve Gretchen's usual—sweetened tea. She took even longer delivering the glass and a menu to the table, all the while avoiding Gretchen's cool gaze. But Valerie had noted an almost feral look in her stone-gray eyes of late. Most likely the woman was still reeling from her landslide loss in the mayoral race last month. Better to avoid that topic altogether.

Valerie plastered on a pleasant look as she slid the glass and the menu before Gretchen. "Would you like to hear the special for the day, Ms. Halifax?"

"I already know it's beef stew, the same thing every Friday." Her voice held a note of contempt.

"Do you know what you would like then?" Valerie asked, keeping her tone friendly even though she wanted to ask why Miss Uppity frequented the greasy spoon if she held it in such low esteem.

The look Gretchen gave Valerie said she wanted to be left alone. "Not yet. I believe I'll just have the tea for now."

"Okay. Let me know when you're ready to order."

Before Valerie could walk away, Gretchen stopped her by saying, "Manny tells me you're from St. Louis."

Valerie wanted to keep walking but instead faced her again. "That was my last place of residence."

"That's quite a long way from Texas."

"Yes, it is."

Gretchen drummed her immaculately manicured fingernails on the table and studied Valerie a long moment. "Why did you come here, of all places?"

Before Valerie could answer, the bell on the door sounded again, saving her from telling another lie. She turned to find that the customer in question was none other than Gavin O'Neal, the interim roommate.

Her heart did an unwelcome jig when he tugged off his jacket and hung it on the coatrack in the corner near the door. Today he looked every bit the lawman in his crisp tailored white shirt sporting the sheriff's department emblem on the sleeve and his light beige cowboy hat. He propped a brown leather boot on the rail beneath one faded red bar stool, his long, jean-clad leg bent at the knee, his badge and holster clipped to his belt loop. He was definitely packing today—enough raw magnetism to melt the glass pie display.

"The sheriff's quite a specimen, isn't he, Valerie?"

Only then did Valerie reluctantly turn back to Gretchen. "He's okay."

Gretchen's smile was as fake as her hair color. "Okay? That's certainly an understatement. But we always want what we can't have, don't we?"

Valerie frowned. "I'm not sure what you mean."

Gretchen clasped her hands together around the glass. "Women like us don't interest men like Gavin O'Neal."

If she only knew. "Why would you think that?"

"Well, I'm too old for him and you—" she sent a derisive glance from the top of Valerie's head to her sneakers "—you're a waitress."

Valerie propped a hand on her hip. "And what's wrong with that?"

"Don't get me wrong, sweetie. I have nothing against the common folk. But Gavin O'Neal's originally from the city. He inherited quite a bit of money. I seriously doubt he would settle for anything less than a woman with proper breeding."

Disgusted with Gretchen's judgment, Valerie braced her palms on the table's edge and leaned into them. "Ms. Halifax, it's character, not pedigree, that counts in the grand scheme of things."

"That sounds nice, but…" Gretchen's voice trailed off as her gaze landed on Valerie's chest. All too late, she knew exactly what the woman had seen. "That's a very lovely necklace."

Valerie clasped the heart pendant and tucked it back beneath the bodice of her uniform. "Thank you. It was a gift."

"It looks to be an antique."

"No. It's made to appear that way." Gretchen's interest in the pendant made Valerie wary. Although she'd worn it since it had come into her possession, she realized it would be best to put it away until she needed it to complete her mission.

Valerie pushed off the table and pulled her pad from her apron pocket and a pencil from behind her ear. "Would you like to order? I highly recommend the stewed prunes Manny prepared especially for Mr. Parker."

Gretchen now focused her attention on the window, specifically on a man standing on the sidewalk, speaking to a woman holding a toddler. "I do believe I've lost my appetite." Without another word she slid from the booth and tossed a five-dollar bill onto the table. "Keep the change. You can use it to get your hair trimmed."

Valerie's hand immediately went to her messy ponytail, subconscious insecurity coming through. She knew better than to let the likes of Gretchen Halifax get to her. As far as Valerie was concerned, the woman's abrupt departure signified good riddance.

After pocketing the money and retrieving the half-empty glass, she turned from the table to find Gavin leaning back against the counter, elbows resting on the Formica surface, legs crossed at the ankles. He looked concerned—and patently gorgeous.

She should give him a good piece of her mind for rearranging her schedule without her permission. She should walk right up to him and tell him to butt out. But what she should do and what she really wanted to do went to war.

Valerie wanted to get in his face all right, but not to scold him. She wanted to kiss him. A real kiss, just to see if his sensual mouth felt as good as it looked. To see if he was as skilled as he was charming.

But work—and common sense—called to her now. And so did Gavin O'Neal.

"Come here, Val." Gavin saw her hesitate a moment prior to striding down the aisle toward him. Before she could hide away in the kitchen, he caught her arm. "Hang on a minute."

She set the glass down and faced him. "What now?"

He countered her frown with a smile. "Just wanted to make sure you're okay."

"I'm fine. Why do you ask?"

"Gretchen has been known to ruin a person's day. She looked like she was giving you a hard time."

She lifted one shoulder in a shrug. "Nothing I couldn't handle. Coffee?"

Here came the game that had evolved between them for the past few weeks. Gavin enjoyed the hell out of it. "You bet."

"Sugar?"

"Sure thing." He tapped his lip. "Right here."

Most times she looked disgusted, but not today when she said, "Lecher."

"Sweetheart."

"Devil."

"Angel."

"Bite me."

Gavin crooked a finger at her, and instead of standing her ground stiff as a board, as she normally did, Val actually moved closer to him. "Name the time and the place and where you'd like that love bite," he said. "And I'll be glad to see to it."

She straightened his collar and patted his chest. "One of these days I'm going to take you up on these questionable offers. Then what are you going to do?"

He toyed with the gold loop in her ear. "Well, since we're in a public place, maybe I should wait to tell you my plans until we're alone. They're kind of detailed."

Valerie's eyes went wide, and Gavin saw it, that flash of desire, of heat, even though she covered it quickly by pointing to the rear of the room. "Sit down and I'll bring you the coffee. If you behave, I'll try not to spill it in your lap." She sent him an overly sweet smile. "Will you be dining alone?"

"I won't be dining at all. Just having a break with friends."

No longer smiling, she propped both hands on her hips. "I live to serve you."

He studied her for a long moment. "Are you mad at me?"

"Let's just say I'm not too happy that you took it upon yourself to ask Manny to give me some time off."

Damn Manny's big mouth. "I thought you could use it. You're wearing yourself out in this place."

She worked her way behind the counter and turned her back to him. "I intend to use the time to find a place to live."

He got the message—loud and clear—and tuned it out. "We can talk about it when I pick you up this afternoon. I'm going to have a seat now."

Without waiting for her response, Gavin took the booth in the rear of the restaurant, away from the windows, the place where he and the other Cattleman's Club members often convened when they weren't meeting at the club itself.

He sat where he could see Valerie, although she still had her back to him, shoving a filter into one coffeepot with a vengeance. She was definitely mad at him, but he wasn't too concerned. Come tonight, he'd try to convince her that he only had her best interest at heart. Maybe he'd give her a peace offering—and he knew just the thing, since she probably wouldn't accept the other offer he had in mind. That involved using their mouths for something other than exchanging barbs.

The door buzzed and Logan Voss strode in. Valerie gave him a smile and inquired about his day, and that ticked Gavin off. Not that he thought Logan had any designs on the waitress. He was too in love with his soon-to-be wife to give any other woman a second look.

"Sorry I'm late," Logan said as he slid into the booth opposite Gavin. "Had to get fitted for my tuxedo."

"Won't be long now," Gavin said. "Are you sure you're ready?"

Logan frowned. "I couldn't be more ready if the wedding happened tomorrow."

Gavin glanced over his friend's shoulder. "Where's Jake? I saw him standing on the sidewalk a minute ago."

Logan chuckled. "I think he's still kissing babies. Someone needs to tell him the campaign's over and since he won, that's not necessary."

"Where are the rest of the guys?" Gavin asked. Only three of the five others currently assisting him in solving Malcolm Durmorr's murder were accounted for.

"Mark's got a self-defense class," Logan said. "He's been booked solid since the announcement that Jonathan Devlin was murdered. Now with Malcolm dead, people are getting nervous, especially the women in town."

"A killer on the loose can do that." Something Gavin had discovered during his tenure as a homicide detective with the Dallas PD. Ironically he'd left that job behind for a quieter life. Now that quiet life involved not one but two murders. "Tom and Rose still honeymooning?"

"Yeah. They'll be back next week. Connor's working on rebuilding the barn that Durmorr burned down."

Before Durmorr had kidnapped Tom's pregnant wife, the sorry bastard. Luckily Rose was safe now, and Gavin was grateful for that even if Durmorr had escaped shortly thereafter, only to end up on the wrong side of a gun. "I'll call Connor and Mark later and catch them up on the investigation."

"We can also talk after the wedding."

Gavin let go a cynical laugh. "Good idea, Voss. I'm sure that will thrill Melissa."

"Just a brief meeting." Logan patted his chest and grinned. "I don't want to put off the wedding night any longer than necessary."

The bell sounded and in walked Jacob Thorne, newly elected mayor. He greeted Valerie, then made his way to the table and slid in beside Logan. "Sorry it took so long. I had some business to attend to."

Gavin grinned. "Still politickin', Jake?"

"Just trying to alleviate a woman's concern about the murders," he said. "So let's get on with it. Chrissie's waiting lunch on me."

Logan and Gavin exchanged a glance before Logan said, "I like a good nooner now and again."

Jake leaned back in his seat. "No kidding. Nothing better than a little afternoon delight with the wife."

Gavin wished they would quit talking about their active sex lives when his was nonexistent. "Okay, then let's get on with it so you guys can get it on with your ladies. I have some information on Malcolm's murder."

All jesting went by the wayside as both Jake and Logan leaned forward, giving their full attention to Gavin. "The preliminary findings show that Durmorr was shot five times," he began. "He took four in the upper torso, including one in the heart, and one in the groin."

Logan and Jake shifted in their seats simultaneously. A dead-aim shot to the jewels gave most men cause to twitch, even though Gavin had seen it before. If the guy hadn't been dead by then, that would've been enough to kill him. "The bullets were .38-caliber. The one in the heart probably did him in. But the one below his belt leads me to believe this was real personal."

"No gun recovered yet?" Logan asked.

"Nope," Gavin said. "Chief Vincente sent out some of the city boys to assist my deputies with scouring the murder scene, but so far nothing. They did find some other interesting evidence on his body. He had several long blond hairs on his jacket."

"Probably from the struggle," Logan said. "Add that to the groin injury and that makes me think a woman killed him."

"I agree with that," Jake added. "And since Durmorr confessed to Rose that he murdered Devlin, my guess is that the killer had something to do with that, too. I can think of one blonde who would be a prime suspect."

So could Gavin, and he'd seen her not more than a few minutes ago. "Gretchen's definitely at the top of my list. But there's something else. The hairs are from two different people. I'm wondering if this was some kind of love triangle gone bad and that it doesn't have a thing to do with Devlin's murder or the presumed hunt for that damn treasure."

Logan shook his head. "Two women? I know Malcolm always considered himself the ladies' man, but it's hard to believe he had one woman, much less two after him."

"Gretchen and Durmorr definitely had something going on between the sheets," Jake said. "Chrissie and I saw them together back in June. We both thought they looked pretty cozy."

A match made in hell, Gavin decided. "She supposedly has an alibi, although I'm going to check that out thoroughly. I imagine she paid off the pizza delivery man to cover for her." He couldn't imagine Gretchen eating pizza.

"Have you talked to Travis Whelan about this?" Jake asked.

Gavin had spoken to the D.A. and former Cattleman's Club member two days ago, and it hadn't been encouraging. "Yeah. He said we've got to have more to warrant a court order for her DNA. Not likely she'll voluntarily hand it over."

"Gretchen doesn't like people telling her what to do, that's for sure," Jake said. "She'll lawyer up right away. You'll definitely need more to go on to make an arrest."

"I plan to keep looking until I find it." And Gavin would, until he had this case solved. "I'd put her under surveillance, but I'm spread pretty thin right now with so many people out sick. Wayne's agreed to help out with some of the city's officers, but he can't cover 24-7. Either of you want to help out a few hours if I decide we need it?"

"The wedding's still a week away," Logan said. "I could do a couple of hours here and there in the next few days, and after the wedding if necessary. We're not going on a honeymoon right now since Melissa's still settling in at the job."

"I can take a shift," Jake added. "As long as it's during the day."

Logan grinned. "And interrupt your nooners?"

"Hey, I perform just as well at night," Jake said.

Time to turn the subject back to the investigation, Gavin decided. "Okay. I'll let you both know if we need some help. I'll talk to Mark and Connor about that, too."

Logan turned and raised his hand. "Could you bring us some coffee now, Valerie? And bring me a piece of Manny's coconut pie, okay?"

"Sure thing, Mr. Voss," Valerie called, a sunny smile on her face. Gavin wished he could earn that kind of smile from her, and someday he would, even if it was the only thing she ever gave him.

"You know, I'm convinced Gretchen did this," Jake said. "But then, I'm probably biased because I saw a really nasty side of her during the campaign."

Logan patted him on the back. "But you came out the victor in spite of that accusation about your campaign defacing her family's historical display. And so far Gretchen hasn't put a hit out on you for crushing her in the election, has she?"

"Not yet," Jake said. "But anything's possible…."

Gavin turned his attention to Valerie, who was pouring coffee and slicing pie. He liked watching her in action. He'd like to watch her in action under different circumstances. Tonight, when he had her alone again, he planned to kiss her soundly, provided she let him do that. Maybe if he played his cards right, she might be willing to play along. It was sure worth a try.

"Are you still with us, Sheriff?"

Gavin snapped out of his waitress-watching to realize Jake had been speaking to him. "Yeah, I'm still here."

"But your mind's on that cute little blonde behind the counter," Logan said, followed by a laugh.

That cute little blonde was heading in their direction, two cups of coffee balanced in one hand, a piece of pie in the other. "Here you go, gentlemen," she said as she slid the fare in front of Jake and Logan.

"Can I get my coffee now, Val?" Gavin asked when she didn't offer him a cup.

"I don't know, *can* you?" she asked.

"May I have it, darlin'?" He topped off the comment with a wink.

She tried her best to look put out, but Gavin noted a smile trying to creep in. Score a point for the sheriff. "I suppose so," she said. "But you'll have to wait until the fresh pot finishes brewing."

"Some things are worth the wait."

Without responding, Val spun around and walked away.

"When are you going to give up, O'Neal?" Logan asked. "That one's never going to come around, I don't care how hard you work on her."

"Believe it or not, she's living with me." Gavin waited for their shock to subside before he added, "At least for the time being."

Logan eyed him suspiciously. "How did you manage that?"

"She was staying in Harvey Joe Raleigh's rental. She had a run-in with him last night over the sorry conditions. She didn't have a place to go, so I offered my guest room."

"And she agreed—" Jake snapped his fingers "—just like that?"

Gavin could leave it at that or he could tell the truth. The truth might work best in case Val should decide to tell the accurate version. "Actually she went after Harvey Joe with a mop and he threatened assault charges. So I told her she could either come home with me or she could go to jail."

Logan barked out a laugh. "That's great, O'Neal. If you can't charm her, then hold her captive in your house. Good plan, even if it does border on coercion."

"I look at it as a little gentle persuasion." Gavin intended to try a lot of that in the next few days, before she left.

Logan regarded Jake. "I give him until the end of the weekend."

"End of tomorrow," Jake said.

Logan held out his hand. "It's a bet."

Gavin knew exactly where this was heading but he chose to

play ignorant. "What's this bet all about and what does it have to do with me?"

"You know damn well what we're talking about, O'Neal," Jake said. "We're betting you have her in your bed real soon."

If only he had their confidence. Gavin wasn't sure he'd even get to first base anytime soon. "If you say so."

"We know so," Logan said before studying Gavin for a long moment, his expression suddenly serious. "Out of curiosity, what do you know about her, Gavin?"

Enough to know that he liked her a helluva lot. "Not much because she's fairly guarded. But I figure she'll eventually open up." When Gavin noticed Logan and Jake exchanging another look, the light suddenly came on. "You're not thinking she's involved in Durmorr's murder, are you?"

"She is blond," Jake said. "And since she attacked Harvey Joe, she might be capable of murder."

"She's been fairly mysterious," Logan added. "Maybe she's a fortune hunter. The woman caught on the surveillance tape stealing the map that's supposed to lead to Jess Golden's treasure was blond with a ponytail. That could have been her."

No way would Gavin ever believe that Val could be involved in anything so heinous. "You're both on the wrong track."

"Maybe you should get a handwriting sample from her and see if it matches the note of apology the culprit left," Jake offered.

Gavin had no intention of doing any such thing. "Val's not the type to shoot anyone over some presumed hidden gold that might or might not really exist."

"If you say so." Logan checked his watch. "And unless we have something else to discuss, I've got to go. More wedding stuff."

"Speaking of the wedding," Gavin said, "mind if I bring a guest with me?"

Logan hooked a thumb over his shoulder. "I take it you mean Valerie."

"Yeah, if she'll agree to go."

"Not a problem," Logan said.

Jake came to his feet. "Good luck with Valerie, Sheriff. It's about time you settled down like the rest of us."

This time shock kept Gavin from speaking for a moment. "I didn't say anything about—" Before he could issue a rebuttal, both Logan and Jake had already tossed a few bills on the table and headed out the door.

Settling down hadn't even entered Gavin's mind to this point. With the demands of his career, he'd never considered that to be a good idea. But when his gaze came to rest on Valerie Raines as she punched the cash register, wisps of golden hair framing her face, her thin eyebrows drawn down in concentration, looking both serious and sexy, he wondered if maybe that wasn't such a bad idea. After he got this murder investigation out of the way, chances were he could go back to patrolling a normally peaceful county. Maybe it *was* time to consider the possibilities. Maybe it was time to find out if Valerie just might be the one to consider. Provided she was still speaking to him tonight.

Three

Valerie had barely changed out of her clothes before Gavin was knocking at the bedroom door. Fortunately Manny had taken pity on her and let her leave the diner early, although she wondered if he'd been persuaded by the sheriff. A very persuasive sheriff.

"Val, are you in there?"

"Just a minute," she called as she pulled the bulky black sweatshirt over her head. When she opened the door, she wasn't quite prepared for the impact of seeing Gavin leaning against the opposite wall, dressed in a white T-shirt covered by a red flannel shirt, his starched jeans replaced by a ragtag pair that had been through the wringer several times.

He straightened and slid his hands into his pockets. "Care to take a little trip with me?"

"That depends on where we're going." Although right now she'd probably accompany him anywhere he'd like to take her, even though she still wasn't happy about his intrusion. She'd told him that again on the way home from the diner, and his response had been no response at all. He'd just grinned, as he was doing now.

When he pushed off the wall, Valerie's heart took a little leap into her throat. "I have something I want to show you."

That sounded very interesting. "What would that be?"

"It's a surprise. You like surprises, don't you, Val?"

Not always. Admittedly this time she was curious. "Okay. You have my attention. Where is this surprise?"

"Outside."

Valerie barely managed to keep up with his long stride as he walked through the great room and out the front door. He turned to his left and strode past the landscaped hedges and up the paved drive to a freestanding garage. He fished a few keys from his pocket and removed several locks securing a heavy chain wrapped around the latch. Once he had that removed, he raised the door, revealing a large object draped in beige canvas, presumably a car.

"What is this?" she asked when he started to pull back the cover.

"You'll see in a minute."

And she did, starting with the taillights before a bright red spoiler came into view. By the time he had the car completely exposed, Valerie could only stare in wonder until she recovered her voice. "Oh my gosh, it's a GTO. What year?"

Gavin dropped the canvas and stood at the hood, looking very proud. "A '69 model."

Valerie walked to where Gavin was standing and asked, "Can I see underneath the hood?"

He looked genuinely perplexed. "Yeah. Sure."

He lifted the hood and secured it with the pins for Valerie to peer inside. "Wow. A four-fifty V-8. I bet it can fly."

"Yeah, if you're so inclined."

She was. "Incredible. It's in mint condition." She looked up to find him smiling. "I don't see you as a classic-car kind of guy."

"It's the size of the engine that gets me going."

She rolled her eyes. "Men and their motors."

He laughed then, a low, compelling laugh. "You can tell a lot about a man if you look under his hood."

She folded her arms across her middle against the sudden bout of chills. "I suppose you're going to say something about the big block."

He forked a hand through his hair. "No, but now that you mention it…"

"Oh, please." She sounded appalled, when in fact she was getting a bit warm just imagining the possibilities. "Do you use it often?"

"The car?"

"Of course I mean the car." However, she still was considering Gavin's personal motor.

"Not often enough these days." His tone bordered on suggestive, and Valerie wasn't about to walk into that trap, even though she was sorely tempted.

"I understand why you would want to limit the mileage," she said. "It increases the value."

"It still needs to be driven, and that's why I want you to drive it until your car is fixed."

"That's very sweet, Gavin, but I can't do that. What if something happens to it?"

"I trust you."

Valerie internally cringed. "You don't really know me."

"I'm getting there."

Oh, but he hadn't come close. "I'm still not sure it's a good idea."

"Why? Can't you handle a stick?"

"Better than most women." And she couldn't believe she'd just said that.

"That sounds interesting." He dropped the hood closed and nailed her in place with his grin. "You don't have to decide to take me up on my offer right now. But I might be tied up when you need a ride. This way you'll have your own wheels."

"Okay, I'll think about it." Truthfully she was dying to get behind the wheel and turn it loose on the rural roads. Probably not a good idea unless she was alone, considering he was authorized to give her a citation.

Gavin narrowed his eyes. "How do you know so much about cars?"

"I spent a lot of time with someone who was fascinated with them. That's all he could talk about." A sixteen-year-old boy she'd counseled. She'd learned all she could about his passion in order to get on his level, hoping to keep him from dropping out of high school, and she had succeeded. A success among the failures.

"He taught you well," Gavin said.

"I'm a quick study. Always have been."

"Good." He wiped his hands on his jeans. "Now you can help me with something."

She pointed behind her. "I thought I might start dinner."

"It's already in the oven," he said.

"Now I'm doubly impressed."

"Don't be. It's frozen lasagna." He turned, strode to a shelf housing several tools and pulled an ax from the top before facing her again. "This shouldn't take that long."

She held up her hands, palms forward. "Okay, I'll drive your car. I'll even clean up after dinner. No need to use that."

He presented his all-star grin. "I'm just going to go out in the back forty and chop some wood for a fire."

Valerie felt somewhat relieved, not that she ever really thought he was going to use the ax on her. "Okay, I can help you with that."

"Don't tell me—you knew someone who taught you how to chop wood."

"No, but again, I learn fast. You just have to show me what to do."

"My pleasure."

A long, tense silence passed before Valerie gathered enough wherewithal to say, "We should get started before the sun goes down."

"Yeah. Let's go."

Gavin led Valerie through a metal gate and onto a parcel of land lined with mesquite trees and brush, bordered on the right by a small creek. The terrain appeared as untamed and rugged as the sheriff did at the moment, Valerie decided after a quick glance in his direction. They walked side by side, the crunch of dried winter grass beneath their feet the only sound interrupting the silence. The atmosphere was very different from her usual surroundings—traffic noises and urban chaos. She breathed in the fresh air untainted by smog. She could get used to this environment, although that wasn't possible. After she'd done what she'd come here to do, she would return to the place she'd called home for most of her life, even if she had no one waiting for her. Even though she would be utterly alone.

"I don't see any cows," she told him as they walked on.

"Haven't had time to build a herd, but I plan to buy a few head in the spring." Gavin stopped at a pile of tangled wood. "I'll just chop some of this up and we can carry it back."

After pulling a pair of gloves from his back pocket and shrugging them on, Gavin raised the ax and landed it squarely on one heavy limb, then hacked it once more until it broke in two. He grabbed up both pieces and laid them to one side.

Valerie stood back, fascinated by his strength, the way he split the limbs with such ease. Everything he did seemed effortless, from his cowboy strut to his charming smile that he now aimed at her.

"Want to try it?" he asked.

"Okay, but I don't think I'm going to be as good at it as you are."

"I've had lots of practice. And you might surprise yourself at that." He propped the ax, blade down, between his knees, pulled off his gloves and offered them to her. "Put these on."

She slid her fingers inside the too-big gloves, suddenly very aware of the difference in their sizes. He had to be at least six-two, and she was barely five-four. His hands were three times as big as hers, and although she sported some muscle, he had solid biceps and triceps and all those "ceps" that mattered most.

He held out the ax handle-first. "It's all yours."

Valerie took the hatchet as well as a deep breath and turned to the pile. "You better stand back, Sheriff. This could get interesting."

She raised the heavy ax high above her head and aimed for one large branch. With all her strength she sliced the wood and received a noisy *thwack,* but the blade wouldn't budge. "It's stuck," she said as she braced her foot on the bough and tugged.

Before she could prepare, Gavin was against her back, reaching around her, one hand resting at the bend of her waist, the other on her wrist. He pulled the ax from the limb easy as you please but still didn't release his grip on her. Valerie glanced back at him. "How did you do that?"

"Let me show you." His voice had a provocative quality, as if he would gladly serve as her guide in any endeavor, both the nice and the naughty.

He lifted her arm and brought the ax back down, splintering the limb in two with only one attempt.

"I don't think I'm cut out for this," she said, her tone laced with frustration. She didn't like to fail at anything.

He pressed closer to her and Valerie froze. "Have you noticed you always seem to be behind me?" she said in a breathless voice.

"Yeah, but I know how to remedy that." He slid his hand up her arm to her shoulder and then brought his lips to her ear. "Put down the ax and turn around."

All the wisdom in the world couldn't stop her from answering his low, compelling command. All the reasons why she shouldn't seemed to float away on the crisp breeze. She lowered the ax to the top of the pile—in slow motion it seemed—and turned into his arms.

"What now?" she asked, although she saw the answer in his dark eyes.

"I'm going to do what I've wanted to do to you since the first day I saw you."

Without even a moment's hesitation he framed her face in his palm and lowered his mouth to hers. Just a kiss, she told herself. Just an uncomplicated kiss—and there was nothing uncomplicated about it. He leisurely parted her lips with his tongue before slipping it inside. He kept it soft, kept it unhurried, kept her pulse fluttering. His palms drifted to her hips, and hers managed to find their way beneath the flannel to the T-shirt.

When he went deeper, explored more fully, Valerie recognized this kiss was an epic occurrence. An experience to be savored. A mind-ripping kiss…that she had to halt now.

Valerie pulled back and brought her hands to his chest, intending to push him back. Instead her palms encountered the corded muscle, the rapid beat of his heart, and she couldn't find the will to take them away.

She'd try a meager protest, about all she could handle at the moment. "We shouldn't be doing this, Gavin."

He surveyed her face before kissing her forehead. "Why not?"

"What will the neighbors think?" And that was quite possibly the lamest thing she'd said in her twenty-seven years.

"First, I only have one real neighbor, and his house is two pastures over." He kissed her cheek. "Second, he's a good friend—Logan Voss—and he wouldn't care." He kissed her other cheek. "Third, even if he did care, that wouldn't matter to me. What just happened between us does matter to me. A hell of a lot." He laid his lips on hers again, kissed her until she felt as if the frozen ground could open up and consume her and she wouldn't really care.

Reality returned, forcing her out of his arms. "It's just not a good idea, us getting involved beyond friendship. I might not be here much longer."

He looked sorely disappointed. "Did you find a new place today?"

"No, not a thing. But I didn't mean at your house, I meant in Royal. I might move on soon."

He slipped his hands in his pockets. "You're the free-spirit sort, huh?"

No, she wasn't. She never really had been, although a few minutes before, she'd felt more liberated than she had in a long time. Maybe even a lifetime. "I'm not sure I fit in here."

"What if I want you to stay a while, both in Royal and in my house?"

Oh, how tempting that would be. "I don't know—"

"Only until after the holidays. Then you can decide." He reached out and stroked her cheek, once chilled from the night air setting in, now warm from his kiss.

She hugged her arms close to her middle. "We should see about dinner now. Hopefully your oven isn't on fire."

He checked his watch. "It still has another twenty minutes, so it's not burning." He raised his gaze to her. "I can't say the same for myself."

She saw the longing in his eyes and she almost fell victim to it. Almost walked back into his arms. Only through sheer resolve did she keep from doing just that. "I need to take a shower before dinner, if that's okay."

"Me, too, so I guess we should head back."

At least he hadn't asked to join her in the shower, although that image came to Valerie in fine detail. Very fine detail.

After he gathered up some wood, refusing her offer to help carry it, they started back to the house, not a word passing between them until they were inside. Only then did Gavin face her. "One more thing you need to know about me, Val."

"What's that?"

"I'm a determined man and I'm going to do everything within my power to convince you to stay."

When he turned and headed toward the hearth, Valerie escaped into the bedroom. She used the closed door for support for a few minutes before she walked to the drawer to retrieve her journal. Her hands trembled when she put pen to paper, but writing her thoughts might make the situation seem less surreal.

Gavin O'Neal offered me the use of his classic car, showed me how to chop wood and kissed me. An amazing kiss that I couldn't begin to describe. It was wrong, but then, it seems everything I've done lately has been wrong. My inability to keep my cool, my questionable plan, my kissing the sheriff. Definitely wrong. Then why does it feel so right?

The sound of clanging bells drew Valerie up the stairs to the loft. She took her time on the ascent, recognizing she should probably turn back around and go to bed. Dinner had been nice, even if a bit tense. That tension should be reason enough to avoid him. But the prospect of spending just a few more minutes in

Gavin's presence kept her going, step by step, until she reached the top. Until she reached him.

Dressed in a black T-shirt covering faded jeans, he stood with his back to her at the pinball machine on the far wall. His brown hair curled slightly at his nape, spurring Valerie's vision of him as a curly-haired toddler who'd probably charmed anyone who'd crossed his path, even back then. He had captivated her from the moment he'd walked into the diner, delivering smiles and compliments as easily as she'd doled out coffee. She'd given him a lot of grief for self-protection, fearing that she would find herself lost to him. And she worried that was exactly where she would be heading if she stayed.

But stay she did, turning her attention to his large hands, so strong and square yet very gentle when he'd held her. His forearms, covered in a fine veneer of golden-brown hair, had prominent veins threaded through them, enhanced by his movements as he worked the machine without mercy. Everything about him was blatantly masculine, and he made her feel incredibly feminine. Before she'd met him, that might have bothered her, yet she was beginning to welcome it. Welcome being in his presence, even if that defied good sense.

Shoring up her courage, Valerie walked to the side of the machine, keeping her hands at her sides in an effort not to smooth the concentration from his face. "Are you winning?"

He aimed his grin on her, a smile calculated to take her breath—and it did. "I am now." Stepping aside, he asked, "Do you want to try it out?"

"I don't want to interrupt your game."

"You won't, so take a shot."

"Okay." She shifted in front of the machine and gave the black plunger a solid pull. The silver ball pinged against the bumpers, and before she could slam it with the flippers, it slipped into the awaiting drain. "I'm not any good at this."

"You just have to concentrate." He moved behind her and slid his arms around her waist. "Anticipate what comes next."

Valerie could almost guess what would come next, and when

Gavin pushed her hair aside, no guesswork was involved. "Your hair smells good," he told her as he nestled his lips against her neck.

This time Valerie pulled back the plunger with so little force, the ball barely rolled an inch. "How am I supposed to concentrate when you're doing that?"

His laughter was low and gruff, effectively sending a series of shivers down Valerie's spine. "Maybe I don't want you to beat me."

"Not much chance in that," she said, trying to ignore the warmth of his breath at her ear, without success.

He braced both palms on either side of the machine and pressed against her. "Okay, I'm not touching you. Try again."

This time she laughed. "What do you mean you're not touching me?" She glanced at him over her shoulder. "You're behind me again."

"Then step away from the machine, turn around and step against me."

Like a susceptible woman in the hands of a master hypnotist, Valerie answered his command. Now they were in full-frontal contact, and she was definitely feeling the effects of his power over her.

She clasped the front of his T-shirt and tipped her forehead against his chest. "I don't understand any of this."

He tugged her head up with his palms, forcing her to contact his lethal dark gaze. "Understand what?"

"Why I'm standing here with Royal's prime catch—who, for some unknown reason, has decided to keep company with someone like me."

"Why not you?"

Any minute now she was going to lose all of her well-rehearsed arguments. "Because we're so different."

"We both like fast cars," he offered.

"And you probably like fast women. Now I know it might appear to you that I fall into that category, but I'm not myself around you."

He didn't look too pleased. "So that's it? You think that I think you're an easy target? A fast woman?"

Precisely. "I wouldn't blame you if you did. I let you kiss me without any argument whatsoever."

"All you have to do is look at me and I'm ready to climb all over you." He tucked her hair behind one ear. "But not once have I ever thought anything but good things about you. Regardless of what does or doesn't happen between us, that's the way it's going to stay."

Guilt sent her gaze away from him. "If you say so, but what I really want is…"

"Tell me what you want, Val."

She forced herself to look at him. "Your respect." And that was the absolute truth.

"I do respect you," he said adamantly. "You're a remarkable woman. Strong. Fun. Sassy. Anything but easy. Definitely sexy."

Sexy? She'd never seen herself that way—except when she was with him. "So when the chase is over, what happens after that?"

His smile warmed her to the core. "Never can tell. I might just decide to keep you."

She didn't believe that for a minute, but all her doubts drifted away, despite the possible consequences, when he laid his lips on hers. His gentle, probing kiss contrasted with the strength of his arms where her hands had landed to anchor herself. She'd never known a man who could be so convincing. Never known a man who could make her feel so very much alive and desirable.

Without missing a beat with the kiss, Gavin picked Valerie up and took her to an unknown destination, and right then she didn't care, even when she felt the hard surface of the poker table beneath her bottom. Only then did he leave her mouth to ask her, "When we're together this way, how do you feel?"

She could give him this truth, even if she couldn't give him her complete trust. "You make me feel things I haven't felt in a long time." If ever.

With one hand he parted the placket of her shapeless oxford shirt and ran a slow finger along her collarbone. "Have you ever thought about us being together this way?"

"Yes." That simple admission took a truckload of effort.

She visually followed his movements as he toyed with the top button on her blouse. "I've thought about it, too," he said. "I've had some serious fantasies about us together. And right now I want the reality. All of it."

So did she, but at what cost? "I'm still not sure this is a good idea."

"Look at me, Val." She raised her head to find him studying her intensely as he rested his palms on her thighs. "Do you want me?"

"I…well…" She couldn't quite voice her feelings, but she recognized that her flushed face, the tiny catch of her breath, gave her away.

He ran a fingertip along her jaw. "That's what I thought."

Gavin held her again, kissed her until all the reasons why she shouldn't allow this flittered away with every soft caress of his lips. With a gentle tug he brought her legs around his waist and her bottom closer to the edge of the table, closer to his body. She ran her hands down his back and up again while his palms drifted along her rib cage beneath the blouse. The kiss turned deeper, wilder, desperate as he grazed his thumbs along the sides of her breasts. She knew that if she only gave him some sort of sign, he'd touch her the way she wanted him to touch her. The way she *needed* him to touch her.

Instead he stilled his hands, broke the kiss and tipped his head against her forehead. "Just say the word, Val, and I'll make love to you. All night. In my bed."

That *word* formed in her mind and came out on a breathy sigh. "Yes."

He lifted his head and leveled his dark eyes on her. "Are you sure?"

"Yes." She covered her face with both hands. "Even though I'll hate myself in the morning."

"Then it's not going to happen tonight."

Totally taken aback, Valerie dropped her hands and stared at him. "I don't understand." And she didn't. First go, then stop. Was he trying to tease her into submission?

He backed up a couple of steps and slid his hands into his

pockets. "I don't want you to hate yourself, and if you do, then you're not ready. And if you're not ready, then I'm not ready."

She sent a direct look at his distended fly. "All evidence to the contrary."

He rubbed a hand over the back of his neck and shifted his weight. "Physically I'm more than ready. But I want you to go into this willingly, without any reservations. And when this happens between us—"

"*If* this happens, you mean."

"*When* it happens, the only thing you're going to feel in the morning is real, real good. Until then, I'm going to let you decide how fast or how slow we go."

She pinched the bridge of her nose between her thumb and forefinger. "This is still a bad idea."

Gavin took her hands into his and rubbed his thumbs along her wrists. "It's not a bad idea at all. It's a great idea. I've wanted you for months now, and if you'll give me the chance, I'll prove how much I want you in ways you won't forget."

She had no doubts about that, even if she did doubt her wisdom in even having this conversation. "You're very sure of yourself, aren't you?"

He brushed her hair aside and kissed her cheek. "I'm only sure of one thing, Val. You're a beautiful, sexy woman and I want you so bad, I hurt. However long it takes to prove that to you, I'm willing to wait. And as soon as we're finally together, neither of us will ever forget it. I promise you that."

Four

Saturday morning arrived, awakening Valerie to guilt. She'd been so shaken by her behavior the night before that she hadn't even written in her journal, as if by putting everything down on paper, she would have to acknowledge her weakness for the sheriff.

She had no idea how she'd let things get so out of hand. Easy. She was drawn to his pure sensuality, as well as everything he stood for as a man. She'd been exposed to enough bad in her lifetime to recognize the good in him. And for that reason she needed to avoid any emotional entanglement.

Still, her grandmother had said she deserved a good man, and Valerie wanted to believe that was true. But the timing was all wrong, and so was any involvement with the sheriff beyond casual friendship. Even that was a stretch, considering her current deception. True friends didn't deceive friends. Right now she had her reasons to keep up the pretense and, under the circumstances, felt she had no other choice.

Valerie waited in her bedroom until she was certain Gavin had left, in many ways afraid to face him, even though she would have to overcome that obstacle at some point tonight. But now she was alone—and she could see a definite advantage in that.

Following a quick shower, Valerie dressed in what she termed her "Saturday sloppies"—baggy blue sweatshirt and threadbare gray sweats. She wandered into the kitchen to find a pot of coffee brewing and a set of keys lying atop a note scribbled in blue ink.

Mornin', darlin'. Feel free to take a drive if you get bored. I'll be all yours tonight.
Gavin.

She poured a cup of coffee and read the note two more times, wishing that he could be all hers. Unbelievable that she would even think such a thing. But she was considering it, considering what it would be like to have him in her life, in her bed every night and every morning. She tucked those thoughts in a secret place that she would never divulge to anyone, especially not the sheriff.

After finishing off the coffee and a piece of dry toast, Valerie sat down and scanned the classifieds for a decent rental that she could afford. Nothing. Now what?

For the past few months she had tried to put together the missing pieces that would complete her mission. She had a copy of the map she had borrowed from the museum display, yet she didn't know the precise location of the Windcroft land, the presumed location of the gold. Coming right out and asking Gavin for directions might seem a bit suspicious at that. She could take his car and try to find the place on her own, but that probably wouldn't be a good idea since the GTO was easily recognizable. She would wait until she had her own car back.

Being a lady of leisure was totally unfamiliar to Valerie, the reason why she liked working at the diner. She had a few hours to fill and nothing to fill them with unless she watched TV. That didn't seem appealing, but taking a tour of the house did. Maybe then she might get to know more about Gavin.

She began with the room immediately off the kitchen that Gavin had designated as his study. As soon as she entered, the heavy weight of guilt settled on her chest. What right did she have to invade his privacy? No right at all, really. But she didn't intend to do anything other than a little minor investigating.

She found only a small desk set across the room, with a lone office chair pushed beneath it. Oddly enough, no computer rested atop of it. In fact, the surface was relatively bare with the exception of an empty in-box. Above that, two shelves housed volumes of what appeared to be mostly books involving crimes, some technical, some fiction and some she had even read herself.

She wasn't cut out for this kind of subterfuge, but that didn't prevent her from seeking another room she had yet to see—although if she'd kept her mouth shut last night, she probably would have seen it.

Valerie bypassed her quarters and opened the door to the room next to hers—Gavin's room. The bed was king-size, framed in heavy oak and covered by a simple black spread. A blue-and-black-plaid sofa sat next to the window, and past that she noticed another door. She decided to take a peek in there first and pushed the door open to reveal an enormous bathroom. Straight ahead, four steps led to a massive whirlpool tub big enough for two, maybe even four, framed by a pair of ivory marble columns, a tall double window providing a gorgeous backdrop. To her right, an L-shaped marble vanity housed a sink, and to her left, an exact replica of the other vanity. Definitely a his-and-hers design. She walked to the sink and simply stared at Gavin's toothbrush, as silly as that seemed, and remembered his mouth in great detail. She picked up his aftershave and gave it a good sniff, then set it down hard, as if she'd been caught going through his little black book. Did he have one?

Valerie shook her head in an attempt to dislodge those thoughts. She couldn't—or shouldn't—be concerned about his love life. She didn't plan to investigate his previous affairs. But in a fit of sheer nosiness, she opened the closet door to find a room bigger than any place she'd ever resided, lit by a high eyebrow window. On one side, several immaculately pressed shirts in white and beige hung from the railing along with a couple of suits, below that a row of slacks and jeans. Several pairs of boots sat lined up on a lower shelf like cavalry soldiers. The opposite side of the closet was bare even though it was built for more clothes. Maybe her clothes? Who was she kidding?

Back in the bedroom, Valerie stopped short of leaving when she noticed the framed photograph set out on the top of the night-stand. She perched on the edge of the mattress and picked up the picture of the man and the woman smiling brightly for the camera. The man had a small cleft in his chin, and the woman had dark, dark eyes. Gavin's resemblance to both was almost uncanny, as if he'd been born with an equal mix of their attributes. She didn't look a thing like her mother and had no idea if she resembled her father since she'd never known who he was. Not even a name or any significant details, and she doubted she would ever know. She doubted her own mother knew for certain.

"That's my parents."

Valerie's gaze zipped to Gavin leaning against the door frame, thumbs hooked in his jeans pockets. Her mortification over being caught in his bedroom was second only to her heated reaction to his presence. Her heart fluttered wildly in her throat, threatening her speech, but somehow she managed to say, "They're a very nice-looking couple."

"Yeah, they were nice. The best."

"Were nice?"

"They're both gone."

The sorrow in his tone, the sadness in his eyes, sent a sharp ache right in the vicinity of Valerie's heart. She decided not to press him for more information since she certainly didn't like people asking too many questions. If he wanted to reveal the details of their deaths, she'd allow him to do that in his own time.

Gavin crossed the room, joined her on the bed and took the picture from her. "My dad had a wicked sense of humor. He was always teasing someone. My mom pretended she didn't appreciate it, but she did."

"You come by that teasing thing honestly, then."

His smile held a certain melancholy that couldn't be ignored. "I guess we're all products of our upbringing."

"I guess that's right." Although Valerie wanted so much to believe that wasn't always the case. Especially for her.

Gavin reached over her and replaced the photo on the nightstand, along with his hat, then laid a palm on her thigh. "You know, if you wanted to see my bedroom, you only had to ask."

She studied her own hands, now clasped tightly in her lap. "I'm sorry. I didn't mean to invade your privacy. I just got a little bored and decided to take a look around. I didn't touch anything other than the picture."

He rubbed her thigh in a slow, sultry rhythm. "I don't mind you looking anywhere you want to look or touching anything you want to touch."

The way he was touching her now had Valerie feeling as if she could go up in flames and come down in a pile of cinders. "What are you doing home? I thought you said you had to work all day."

He stopped his soft stroking but kept his hand firmly planted on her leg. "Actually I came by to drop off the rest of your things. I went by Harvey Joe's and picked them up."

Panic constricted Valerie's chest. "You didn't have to do that. I would have gone back in a day or two."

"Not a problem. You don't have all that much, unless I just didn't see everything."

Hopefully he *hadn't* seen everything. "Only some clothes and a couple of boxes."

"Yeah, that's what I brought with me. I put your hanging things in the closet and the stuff from your drawers on top of the box of books." He studied her a long moment, causing her to look away. "I noticed they were college textbooks."

So much for pretending she'd been a lifelong waitress. "I went to the local university for a while, but after my grandmother died, I had to quit." Not exactly a lie, even though she did have her undergraduate degree and was well into working on her master's. But if she told him that, then he would wonder why she hadn't pursued her career in St. Louis instead of settling in Royal.

"I noticed the books had mostly to do with psychology," he said.

"Yes. The human mind fascinates me."

Gavin's smile turned into a grin. "Me, too. Almost as much as the human body."

Valerie's all-too-human body was making itself known with a racing pulse and a rolling heat. "Why does this not surprise me?"

"Guess it shouldn't surprise you at all after last night." He lifted his hand from her leg and draped his arm over her shoulder. "And about that, I owe you an apology for pressuring you."

"You didn't pressure me," she said.

"Yeah, I did." He stroked his thumb along her jaw. "But I have to admit, I've thought about it all day long."

Gavin got that look about him, the one that told her he was about to kiss her. And he did, with gentle yet effective persuasion that had Valerie opening to him without hesitation and leaning toward him as if he had power over her like the moon over the tides. The things he could do to her with his mouth were beyond anything she had ever known. The way she responded was totally out of character for her normally cautious self. She welcomed the soft stroke of his tongue and met it with her own, enjoyed the feel of his hand traveling from her waist to her hip and back up again.

"I don't have time to do this right now," he murmured as he feathered soft kisses along her neck and down the column of her throat.

"Then leave before…"

He raised his head and stared at her. "Before what?"

"Before I can't let you leave."

He pushed off the bed, forked one hand through his hair and let go a rough sigh. "You're killing me, Val."

"Sorry, that wasn't what I meant to do at all. And I believe you started it by kissing me first."

He took his hat from the nightstand and placed it on his head. "Yeah, and we're going to have to finish it soon or I might be forced to permanently reside in the company vehicle to preserve my dignity, if you catch my meaning. Kind of hard to do when you're out on a call." Leaning over, he gave her a quick kiss. "I've left some money for you in the kitchen in case you need it."

"I'll probably pick up something for dinner at the store, but I have my own money."

"Keep your money. An even trade if you'll do the shopping." Before Valerie could argue that buying food was a fair exchange for the room, Gavin left, calling, "I'll see you tonight when I get home."

Valerie collapsed back onto the bed and rested one palm over her pounding heart. In Gavin O'Neal's company, she was as weak as a sapling tree and as foolish as a teenager. The longer she stayed, the deeper involved she might become. But she couldn't resist him anymore than she could change who she was, and that created a terrible dilemma.

Gavin pulled up in front of the post office, left the SUV running and hurried inside, thankful to be out of the less-than-pleasant elements, at least for the time being. He walked up to the window and rang the bell, waiting for several minutes for Abe to get out of his chair and shuffle to the counter.

"Howdy, Sheriff," the man said with a smile, revealing a set of yellowed dentures. "What can I do for you?"

"Harvey Joe Raleigh told me he sent some mail back that belongs to Valerie Raines. Do you know where it might be?"

Abe rubbed his stubbly chin. "Let me look. It might take a while."

Gavin didn't doubt that for a minute. "I'll wait."

Leaning one elbow against the counter, Gavin turned and stared out at the deserted street. Everyone had taken shelter from the bitter cold, with good reason. The forecast called for a winter storm due to arrive in a matter of hours, bringing with it the threat of snow. An unusual occurrence for this time of year for Royal, or so he'd been told, but not completely unheard of. If he had his way, he'd stay in for the night with his houseguest, alone, and get to know her better. And it would probably be best not to think too much about that now. He'd had one heck of a time blocking the images of her on his bed where he'd left her that morning. He'd had an even harder time erasing the fantasies of seeing her there again, this time naked. Hell, he was having a hard time, period.

He turned back to the window and peered inside to find Abe working his way through a stack of mail at a snail's pace. At this rate, it might be midnight before he went home to Valerie, and that wouldn't do. The sound of the opening door turned Gavin around to discover another blonde entering the building. She pulled her black leather coat closer to her body when she contacted his gaze.

"Hello, Sheriff." Her tone was as cold as the rush of air that had followed her inside.

He tipped the brim of his hat. "Gretchen. Haven't seen you around much lately."

Her gaze slid away. "I've been busy."

Now that she'd lost the mayor's race, Gavin couldn't imagine what was keeping her so busy. He guessed shopping and extolling the virtues of a stellar bloodline were time-consuming. Right then, he had a prime opportunity to ask a few questions in an informal setting. "I don't think I've told you that I'm sorry about your friend's death."

She raised one thin eyebrow. "Friend?"

"Malcolm Durmorr."

After pulling off her leather gloves, she rifled through her purse, avoiding his scrutiny. "I wouldn't exactly call him a friend."

Gavin leaned back against the counter. "From what I hear, you two were pretty tight at one time."

She withdrew a stack of envelopes and clutched them in her fists. "You can't always believe what you hear in this town, Sheriff."

And he didn't believe her for one minute. "I guess that's true. By the way, where exactly were you the night that he died?"

Her expression turned to steel. "As I told one of your deputies, I was at home. You can ask the pizza delivery man."

"Anyone else see you after he left?"

A flash of hostility clouded her eyes, but she kept her tone even when she said, "Why? Am I a suspect?"

The number-one suspect, as far as Gavin was concerned. "When it comes to a murder case, everyone's a suspect."

"Does that include Valerie Raines?"

Now where in the hell had that come from? "You know I can't reveal any details, but is there any reason why she would be?"

"Because Malcolm told me she threatened him once in the diner."

"Threatened him?"

"Yes, with a fork. I believe he might have asked her out on a date. I told him he should steer clear of her, but for some reason she fascinated him. There is absolutely no accounting for taste."

"Are you sure he didn't do more than ask her out?"

She shrugged. "I'm not sure, but I doubt whatever he might have done warranted a threat. However, I suspect Ms. Raines has quite a temper. She just manages to hide it well."

Gavin had seen a hint of that temper, but he honestly didn't believe she would take someone's life. "I think you have her pegged wrong."

She sent him a devious smile. "Why don't you question her about it? It's my understanding she's living with you."

Damn the small-town grapevine. "Well, Gretchen, like you said, you can't always believe everything you hear."

"Here you go, Sheriff," Abe said, prompting Gavin to turn. "Only a couple of pieces, but you might have Miss Raines come down and put in a forwarding address so nothing gets lost. Or you could do it since it's your address."

Damn. "Thanks, Abe. I'm in a hurry right now."

"I suppose you *can* believe what you hear," Gretchen said from behind him.

Talk about bad timing, Gavin thought as he faced her again. "Just helping out a friend, Gretchen. That's all."

Her eyes went as cold as the ice forming on the window. "Of

course. Whatever you say. But I wouldn't trust that waitress any farther than I could toss her."

And Gavin didn't trust Gretchen Halifax any farther than he could hurl his thousand-acre spread. "Have a nice evening, Gretchen. And one more thing."

She cocked her head and leveled a hard stare on him. "What would that be?"

"Don't leave town anytime soon."

Without waiting for a response, Gavin pushed out the door and back into the frigid conditions. The sound of a revving engine turned his focus to the street and an approaching car. His dad's car, to be exact. And behind the wheel, a waving waitress who obviously possessed a lead foot. At least she'd slowed when she passed.

Tonight he would have to give Val a mild scolding for speeding, if only for the sake of her safety. And no doubt about it, he planned to give her a long, long kiss.

"Something smells real good."

Valerie looked up from the stove to discover Gavin hanging his hat and his coat on the hook by the back door. Her heart immediately started the confounded fluttering, as if she'd consumed several shots of potent espresso or Manny's morning coffee.

She gave the pot a stir, then covered it again without turning around. "It's chicken and dumplings, my grandmother's recipe. I went to the store today and picked up a few things after you left."

"So that's where you'd been when you came flying into town."

She looked back to catch his grin. "I wasn't flying." Just speeding a little. After pulling the hot pads from her hands, she faced him. "I wanted to get home to start dinner so you wouldn't have to wait. Plus, the weather was starting to look kind of shaky. I didn't want to get caught out in it." And luckily he hadn't caught her after she'd left town for wide-open spaces. She hadn't topped ninety, but boy had she wanted to.

He pulled back a chair at the dinette, turned it around and straddled it. "It's more than shaky outside right now. It's snowing."

Valerie headed for the window and pulled back the curtain. A thickening blanket of white covered the pasturelands, reminding her of one bitter winter when she'd been colder than she'd ever been in her life. The same winter she'd made a terrible mistake that had almost cost her dearly.

Pushing those recollections away, she stared at the flurry of fat flakes. "Wow. It's beautiful. I love snow." As long as she had some place warm to go. In this instance, that place was in Gavin's house. In Gavin's arms.

"They've forecasted six to eight inches," he said.

"Six inches would be good, but eight's even better." When she heard Gavin's low chuckle, she turned and pointed at him. "Don't even say it."

He put his hands up, palms forward. "I didn't say a thing."

"But you were thinking it."

He leaned forward and clasped his hands in front of him on the table. "Actually I'm thinking I'm about to starve. When's dinner going to be ready?"

She checked the clock on the wall. "In about ten minutes. And after dinner I want to play."

He held her completely captive with his sultry smile. "I wouldn't mind that one bit, playing after dinner."

She couldn't suppress her own smile. "I meant in the snow. We can build a snowman."

"We could sit by the fire."

"*After* we build the snowman."

"Okay. I can wait that long."

If Valerie knew what was good for her, she'd hightail it to her room after dinner and avoid him. But she only knew that Gavin O'Neal had enough heat in his brown eyes to melt what snow had already fallen—and all of her arguments to stay away from him.

As well as she knew her feelings for the sheriff were steadily growing, she also knew that if he found out about her previous mistakes, he might not give her another look or another chance, just like the other man in her life. Her legacy would be laid bare for everyone's judgment and she would be labeled a fortune hunter, even if she wanted answers, not riches. Again she would be forced to face the shame. No one would see her in the same light. The townspeople would no longer respect her as they did now—Valerie, the friendly waitress who had no past as far as they were concerned. No one would understand, especially not Gavin. Or would he?

Later tonight she might put him to the test by revealing she descended from a line of lawless women, even if she couldn't quite tell him that many years ago she'd crossed the line herself. And depending on how that went, maybe she would confess her real reasons for being in Royal.

Yes, Gavin would understand. He had to, otherwise her heart would surely shatter.

"Are you sure you want to do this, Val?"

"Yes, as soon as I'm ready."

Gavin was ready—to dispense with all formality and grab her. He'd sat across from her at dinner, concentrating on her mouth while he'd watched her eat. He'd helped her clean up, brushing against her every chance he got. Now he had a great view of her butt as she bent over a box she'd shoved into the closet.

Val still insisted on playing in the snow, when he had a different kind of play in mind. Foreplay.

"I found it," she announced as she straightened, clutching a pink knit cap that matched a pair of pink knit gloves.

She tossed the winter wear onto the bed before righting the mess she had made while rifling through the box. Gavin caught sight of a black baseball cap, and for a split second he was struck by a familiarity that he didn't understand. Then he remembered. The culprit they'd caught on the surveillance camera at the museum had been wearing a black cap. And a ponytail.

Not Valerie. He couldn't imagine her pilfering a map. Besides, what would she want with that? Unless she was also searching for the gold.

Nah. If that were true, she would've been out looking instead of working in the diner. She wouldn't be in his house, cooking him dinner and keeping him highly entertained. But then again, she had been out today, in his dad's car. She would've had the opportunity....

Gavin shoved those thoughts from his mind, hating that his friends had unintentionally planted them there. Val was a good woman. He knew that just as he knew every back road in the county.

Finally she stood and took the down coat he'd offered her. "You don't need this jacket?"

"Nope. It's a spare."

"Great." She piled her ponytail beneath the cap, wriggled her fingers into the gloves, then put on his jacket that practically swallowed her whole. "All right. Let's go have some fun."

Tromping around in below-freezing weather in several inches of snow that had yet to let up wasn't necessarily Gavin's idea of a good time. But he'd never seen Val quite this enthusiastic before and he wouldn't dare do anything to quell that right now. After all was said and done and she'd had her fill of the brutal conditions, he planned to warm her up and hopefully generate some heat and a little more excitement.

He followed her down the hall, watching every step she made as she swayed into the kitchen. He grabbed his own coat off the hook by the back door and barely had it on before she was sprinting down the steps and out into the yard.

He found her twirling around, flakes raining down on her up-turned face. "I love this!"

Gavin loved the way she looked at the moment, with her cheeks flushed and her eyes alight with pure joy. Her carefree pleasure was contagious. But he didn't care too much for her sudden need to fling a few snowballs at his unprotected head. He went to grab her, but she was too quick, and he ended up flat on his ass in a mound of slush.

"You're going to pay for this," he shouted. And she would, provided he could catch her.

Finally he did, but he soon recognized she'd wanted to be caught. She didn't put up much of a fight when he tugged her against him and held her tight. She didn't complain when he kissed her, her lips cool àgainst his but quickly warming as he took her mouth in earnest.

Only the sound of the whistling wind interrupted the stillness of the night, and as far as Gavin was concerned, nothing could stop him from laying claim to her lips for the rest of the evening, provided Val agreed. She was certainly being agreeable now.

When he felt his hands numbing beneath his leather gloves, Gavin finally pulled away. "Have you had enough yet?"

She sent him a coy look. "Of the snow or your mouth?"

"Definitely the snow."

"I guess it is a little chilly out tonight. But I didn't notice it too much a few seconds ago."

"Neither did I." He brushed some frozen powder off her face and kissed the tip of her nose. "But I'm about to freeze where I stand, so why don't we take this inside?"

She pretended to pout. "No snowman?"

"Tomorrow, if it sticks."

"It will." Then she reached down to scoop up more snow, formed another frozen missile and tossed it at his chest before she rushed inside the house. He found her in the kitchen, winded with laughter and shaking out her hair. She didn't only look cute at the moment. She looked beautiful.

"I'm going to put on some dry clothes now," she said as she took a few steps backward.

He wanted to offer to remove her clothes and keep her warm. Real warm. "I'll meet you in front of the fire."

She shimmied out of the jacket. "Good. Then maybe I'll finally get warm."

"I'll warm you up. I guarantee it."

"I'm counting on it." Smiling, she turned toward the hall while Gavin pulled off his own jacket. He needed to change, too, and he could very well change into a raving lunatic if she didn't quit tempting him. As he passed her bedroom, he heard whistling from behind the closed door, followed by the sound of laughter.

Gavin knocked and called, "You need something, Val?"

She cracked the door open just enough to give him a glimpse of bare shoulder. "I just might, but I guess you'll have to wait and see, won't you?"

After she shut the door in his face, Gavin shook his head and leaned back against the opposite wall. She was the damnedest thing he'd ever seen and the most incredible woman he'd ever met. Instinctively he'd known that about her since they'd met and he couldn't imagine ever getting tired of being around her. In fact, he needed to be around her about as much as he needed his morning cup of coffee.

He could only hope that someday she might begin to trust him. Need him as much as he was beginning to need her. Maybe even tonight.

Five

"The fire looks great, Sheriff."

Crouched before the hearth, Gavin glanced back to see Valerie standing behind him, wearing the oversize shirt covering some sort of skin-hugging top and a pair of loose-fitting blue-striped pajama bottoms. Her hair hung down around her shoulders, reflecting the fire and making it look like a fall of gold. Although he should take this slowly, slowly didn't seem at all interesting. In fact, he could have her on the floor in two seconds flat and her clothes off her in about five.

Get a grip, O'Neal.

He straightened and faced her, keeping a safe distance—for the time being. "It took a while, but now it's going full force." So was he.

She clasped her fingers together and straightened her arms before her. "I love a good fire."

He loved the way she looked right then, all soft and feminine. But she also looked a little worried. "Why don't we have a seat and enjoy it for a while?"

"Sure," she said, surprising Gavin with the ease of her agreement.

"Over here." He moved the coffee table aside to allow a full view of the hearth, then sat on the rug with his legs stretched out before him and his back to the couch.

She hovered over him, sporting a severe stare. "Do you have an aversion to sofas?"

"Nope. I just happen to like sitting on the floor." He patted the space beside him. "Try it. You might like it."

"Okay." She lowered herself beside him, keeping a moderate berth between them, and hugged her knees to her chest. "You know what you need?"

Oh, yeah, he did. But he decided not to voice that right now. "What do I need?"

She surveyed the room for a minute. "You need a Christmas tree." She pointed to the window that faced the front yard. "Right there. A big tree with lots of lights and ornaments."

A host of bittersweet recollections flooded Gavin's mind, followed by those so tragic that he'd made a concerted effort not to think about them too often. "I'm not one to decorate."

"Why not? It's a wonderful tradition. Some of my best memories are holiday memories."

Some of Gavin's were his worst. "Do you prefer real or artificial trees?"

"Definitely real ones, although I learned a long time ago that you can improvise if you need to." She curled her legs to one side and shifted to face him, one arm resting on the sofa's cushions. "When I was little, we didn't have much money, so we never had a real tree. But when I was about nine, I talked one of my teachers into letting me make my own tree out of construction paper and poster board. From that point forward it became a tradition. My grandmother made sure that tree was on the wall every year, right after Thanksgiving."

Finally he knew a little about her life, and that drove him to want to know more. "What about your mom and dad?"

She studied her sock-covered feet, avoiding his gaze. "My

mother and I are estranged. I haven't seen her for years. My father's never been involved in my life."

At least Gavin had known the love of two parents, even if they'd been torn from his life all too soon. "Where's your grandmother now?"

He noted an immediate sadness in her expression. "She passed away last year. That's one of the reasons I set out on my own."

He was curious about the other reasons, but decided not to push her. "I'm sorry, Val. It's tough losing family."

"Yes, it is." She looked up and gave him a soft smile. "Did you have traditional holidays when you were growing up?"

"Yeah, we did. My mom was really into tradition before she passed away."

"How long ago was that?" Val asked.

"In two weeks, it will be seventeen years since they died."

"Your parents died at the same time?" Her tone reflected her shock. "How?"

Gavin had two options—to change the subject or to tell her the details behind his parents' deaths. Normally he would shut down about now, but for some reason, he thought she might understand. Maybe he could release some of the burden that this time of the year always brought him. "They came home from a Christmas party and surprised two intruders. They didn't survive."

Val released a slight gasp. "They were—"

"Murdered." Saying it still didn't make it any easier for Gavin to accept. "Both shot, all because of greed."

"Did they catch the killers?"

"No." He released a long sigh and stared straight ahead. "I was in college in East Texas at the time. I stayed on campus for a function, otherwise I would have been home that night. For years I wondered that if I had been home, would things have turned out differently."

"Or you could have been a victim, too," she said. "Sometimes it's best not to question those things, the whys and hows, especially if we can't change anything."

How many times had he told himself that very thing? To this

point, it hadn't worked. "I guess you're right, but it's tough to forget."

"I'm sure it is. And something tells me that's why you went into law enforcement."

Val's speculation didn't surprise Gavin. He'd sensed her intuitiveness from the beginning. "Yeah. I changed my major from business to criminal justice. I went to work for the Dallas PD and made detective in a relatively short time. I worked the worst cases, mostly homicides, until I finally got tired of fighting a battle that I couldn't win." And searching for his parents' killers in his spare time, without success.

"But you couldn't stay away from it, could you?"

Gavin glanced Val's way to find her staring at him. He focused on the fire to avoid her assessment. "Initially I wanted to give it up, so I bought this place and moved here. I intended to ranch, but they needed deputies, so I signed on to do that part-time. A few months later the sheriff decided to retire. He convinced me I needed to replace him, so I threw my name into the hat thinking someone else with more tenure who liked politics would run against me. Didn't happen, so back in May I became the sheriff of Royal by default, I guess you could say."

"You don't sound that happy about it," she said.

She could read him well. Too well. "I'm not unhappy. Just frustrated that I'm knee-deep in serious crime again with the second murder investigation in six months. But I'm going to solve this case. I don't have a damn bit of tolerance for criminals of any kind."

Val folded the hem of her shirt back and forth. "What about crime because of necessity?"

"I don't see the necessity in any kind of crime." His tone was adamant, almost angry. But lawlessness generally pissed him off.

"Even if someone was, say, stealing food because they had no money?" she asked. "I've seen kids who've gotten into trouble because they were simply hungry."

He'd seen much worse than that. "No excuse. If parents cared more about keeping their kids in line, crime would go down. But then you also have to consider that it's common for criminals to produce criminals, and that's a real problem."

She stared at him long and hard, a hint of anger in her eyes. "Then you honestly believe it has to do with genetics instead of nurturing?"

He didn't like the course of this conversation one whit, but he had to stand his ground. "I think it's a combination of both. But I've seen it too many times, kids who follow in their parents' footsteps. Fourteen-year-old kids who learn to steal and even some who kill. It makes me sick inside. Unfortunately there doesn't seem to be anything that works to stop it."

She lifted her chin a notch. "I think you're wrong about that. I believe people can change if they have the proper guidance."

He shrugged. "Maybe so, but I'm jaded because of everything I've witnessed as a cop." Something he wouldn't wish on anyone, especially Val. "And I don't expect you to understand because you're such a good woman."

She remained quiet for a long moment before she said, "I'm not perfect, Gavin. I've made my share of mistakes."

"Haven't we all?" He took her hand into his. "Whatever mistakes you've made—and I doubt they amount to much—don't matter to me. In fact, I don't even care to know about them. As far as I'm concerned, no good comes from rehashing the past."

She raised her gaze from their joined hands to his eyes. "Then you're saying you're wiping my slate clean of all mistakes?"

"That's exactly what I'm saying."

Her smile arrived slowly, melting the last of his latent anger. "You're pretty tough, Sheriff. But in a way I can understand why you feel the way you do. If I'd lost someone I'd loved in such a horrible way, I'd probably feel the same way, too."

He saw sincere understanding in her eyes and he knew he hadn't been wrong in sharing his past with her. "I've never told one soul in Royal about my parents' deaths, aside from you. I've never wanted to tell anyone before you."

"And you can trust me not to repeat it," she said. "But I am surprised you haven't confided in your friends. They seem trustworthy."

"They are, but it's not something I like to discuss."

"Because it still hurts," she said in a simple statement of fact. "I understand." She sounded as though she truly did.

"How about we talk about something else?" Anything else would do, as far as Gavin was concerned.

She stretched her legs out before her. "Okay. I have a question for you. Exactly what do you and your friends talk about in that corner booth at the diner? The way you all huddle together, one might think you're plotting and planning something."

She was definitely close to the truth. Many a member of the Cattleman's Club, both past and present, had done that very thing in that very booth, or so he'd been told when they'd asked him to join their elite club. But they'd all been sworn to secrecy when it came to their missions. "Basically we shoot the breeze. Talk about our jobs and pastimes, that sort of thing."

Val sent him a full-fledged grin that would have knocked the floor out from under his feet if he hadn't already been sitting on it. "Maybe plotting the seduction of unsuspecting women?"

"Yeah, that has come up in the past, but not for a while now. All of the guys in the group are presently attached. Except for me."

She pulled a throw pillow from the sofa and circled her arms around it. "I still have a hard time believing you haven't found the right woman."

He hadn't really been looking. Until now. "A lot of women are turned off by the demands of my job, or so I've been told."

"Your merciless teasing could also be a deterrent."

He tugged the pillow from her clutches and tossed it back on the couch. "I reserve that behavior only for you."

"Should I be flattered?"

He pushed her hair away from her shoulders and nuzzled his face in her neck. "Yes, you should definitely be flattered, darlin'."

"You're a class-A scoundrel."

He brought his lips to her ear. "I try, sweetheart."

"The consummate bad boy."

"But I can be real good."

"Bi—" She glanced away. "Never mind."

"Okay." Gavin took her earlobe between his teeth, applying only light pressure. When she shivered and sighed, he wrapped an arm around her and asked, "Are you cold, Val?"

"No."

"Neither am I." He cupped her jaw in his palm. "In fact, I'm downright hot."

He proved that to her with a hot kiss, taking her mouth without pause, all the while warning himself to take it easy. But *easy* wouldn't adequately describe the way she responded to him, meeting his tongue with sultry strokes that threatened his declining control.

For a time he was content with just having one arm wrapped around her, his hand tangled in her hair. But that was short-lived when she leaned closer and rested her arm across his belly. He slid his palm up her arm and tugged the baggy shirt down her shoulder to give him better access. Leaving her mouth, he worked his way along her neck, then back up again. He wanted that damn shirt gone. He wanted a lot more than he probably should.

Good sense told him to back off, but he couldn't lay claim to any sense at the moment. He made his way back to her mouth, wanting her closer. Needing her closer. With little effort he lifted her onto his lap to straddle his thighs. He broke the kiss to look at her—hair mussed and flowing around her face, eyes hazy. She locked her gaze firmly into his when he slid the shirt off her shoulders and down her arms, leaving her wearing only the tight knit top. He saw no signs of protest in her expression, no fear or hesitation. Against better judgment, he scooted down and bent his knees, sending her directly against his erection. Right now he didn't care. He wanted to be that close to her even if clothing provided a barrier he preferred to be gone.

With one hand on her nape, he brought her lips back to his and kissed her while he worked his hands beneath the back of the skimpy tank. No bra as an obstacle, only the smooth texture of bare flesh against his palms. He curled his hands around her sides and moved them up then down. He broke the kiss to watch her face as he grew bolder, using his thumbs to stroke the sides of her breasts.

She didn't tell him to stop, didn't push him away, and that gave him the courage to say, "I need to see you."

Gavin pulled his hands from beneath the top and clasped the thin straps. He slid them down slowly, giving her another chance to stop him, but she didn't. She did keep her arms at her sides until Gavin lifted them, one at a time, to remove the straps completely. With his gaze firmly locked with hers, he lowered the top to her waist, baring her to his eyes and then to his hands.

He kept his strokes light, playing her pale pink nipples gently between his thumb and forefingers. Val still hadn't said a word, but the broken quality of her breathing, the pleasure in her eyes, told Gavin all he needed to know. She was enjoying this, and so was he. But when her hips began to move in an erotic rhythm against his groin, that was just about more than he could stand.

He braced his hands on her bottom to halt her and, on afterthought, worked her off his lap and laid her back on the rug. After whipping his own shirt over his head and hurling it away, he stretched out partially atop of her. He kissed her again as he rubbed his chest against her breasts, savoring the feel of her against him. A long time had passed since he'd been this close to a woman, feeling her heart beat rapidly against his. But then, a long time had come and gone since he'd wanted to be this close to a woman, other than Val.

Gavin left her mouth to look at her, seeing what he wanted to see—needed to see—in her expression. Her eyes remained closed but her bottom lip trembled as she shifted beneath him again. He found the pulse at her throat with his mouth and then kissed his way down her throat to the cleft between her breasts. Without hesitation, he drew a nipple into his mouth, using his tongue to caress her, to taste her, even knowing that in a matter of minutes he'd want more than just the foreplay. He'd want it all.

Before that could happen, he had to know if she wanted it, too. Without any misgivings or possible regrets. He raised his head and looked at her straight on. "Tell me to stop now, Val, before I can't."

Her eyes drifted open and she shook her head. "I don't want you to stop."

He experienced a rush of relief, but he still needed more confirmation. "If we keep going, you're not going to hate yourself in the morning, are you? You're not going to hate me?"

She slid her finger down his jaw. "I'll never hate you, Gavin. I'm ready for this to happen. I promise."

That was all he needed to know. But as he lowered his mouth back to hers, the grating sound of his portable radio echoed in the room.

"Sheriff O'Neal, highway patrol needs assistance working an MVA on Route 16."

Before Valerie could respond with her own aggravated oath, Gavin leaned his forehead against her shoulder and muttered, "Dammit."

"Do you copy, Sheriff?"

He sat up, retrieved the handheld radio from the coffee table and depressed the button. "Yeah, I copy. I'll be there in ten."

After setting the radio down hard, Gavin stared at her, looking more than a little displeased and a whole lot frustrated. But then, so was Valerie. "Obviously I have to go."

Valerie grabbed her top and held it against her breasts, thinking fate was having a fine time keeping them apart—and probably with good reason. "Will it take long?"

He grabbed his shirt and tugged it over his head while she did the same. "I don't have any idea. Depends on how many cars are involved and the extent of the injuries. Traffic control in these conditions is important, otherwise we could have a major pileup."

Valerie couldn't deny her own disappointment even though she understood why he had to go. Maybe this *was* some sort of sign, a warning that she should reconsider what she had almost done. What she still wanted to do—make love with him. "I'll be here when you get back."

"And I'll be back as fast as I can." Gavin came to his feet. "If

I know you're waiting for me in my bed, that will make doing my job a whole lot easier."

"I'll think about it." And she would, long and hard.

He leaned over and gave her another deep kiss, then he was gone out the kitchen door before Valerie had the presence of mind to move. After a time she stood and walked down the hall on weak knees, engaging in a serious mental debate all the way to her designated bedroom.

She hadn't been able to tell him the truth once she'd recognized that he couldn't accept her past in light of his convictions when it came to crime. But he'd said that her mistakes didn't matter to him. He'd also said he didn't want to know about them, and maybe that was best. In his eyes, she was only Valerie, a woman worth knowing. A woman he desired. A woman with no past.

In Gavin's arms, she hadn't cared about the pros and cons of getting involved with him. She'd only cared about the way he'd made her feel. She only cared that for once in her life, she'd felt truly free to explore her own sexuality without reservation.

Pushing all caution aside, she decided to wait in his bed for his return. Wait to enjoy a few stolen moments, a sweet respite from that past, before she left him for good—and hope that someday he would forgive her and understand why she couldn't tell him. Why she needed him to see her in a good light before he learned about the bad.

Before she went to his room, she still had one thing left to do. As always, she turned to her nightly writing to sort things out, her hands trembling as she retrieved the journal.

It's going to happen between us, regardless of all the reasons it shouldn't. When Gavin returns, I'm going to be waiting in his bed and I'm going to enjoy every moment of his lovemaking. I'll file the memories away and bring them out when I'm no longer with him. Right now I can't even consider being without him, and that is more risky than what I have left to do.

At 6:00 a.m. Gavin walked through the back door and went straight for his bedroom. Fortunately he'd had a ten-minute drive and cold weather before he'd reached the accident to aid him in his recovery following his interlude with Val. He'd also had the reality of a two-car wreck with multiple injuries to get his mind off her and onto business. Clearing the carnage had taken longer because of the conditions, and luckily no one had been killed.

On the drive to the accident site he'd remembered what he hadn't had available in the house—condoms—so the interruption had probably been for the best. And the lone convenience store on the way back to the ranch didn't open until seven, so he would just have to wait until later to prepare. Another intrusion directly resulting from his job. But come hell or more highway mishaps, he was going to make love to her tonight, even if he had to toss his radio down the old well out back.

Even if he couldn't have her this morning, he was still curious to see if Val had followed his instructions. When he reached his room, he found her there, curled on her side away from him, the bedcovers bunched at her feet as if she'd been restless most of the night. He could definitely relate to that, especially now when he saw she still wore the same too-big shirt and nothing else aside from a pair of sheer white panties. He had a bird's-eye view of her bottom, and, although he was dog tired and needed some sleep before he had to go into the office in a few hours, his body came back to life at the sight.

Caution crept in, sending Gavin to the bed, where he tugged the sheet over Val, then made his way to the opposite side. He could go to one of the guest rooms or to the couch or he could stay strong, stay in control and climb in beside her. After all, he didn't have to touch her. He just had to develop an iron will.

With that thought, he tugged off his T-shirt and pulled off his boots and socks but left his jeans on. Stripping down to his briefs might prove to be too tempting, even if his pants were more than a little tight at the moment. As quietly as he could, he slipped into the bed and stretched out on his back, remaining on top of the covers. He glanced at Val, relieved that he hadn't woken her, because if she made one move toward him, he might forget about sleep and the reasons why they couldn't finish what they'd started last night.

He laid one arm behind his neck, rested his other across his bare abdomen and closed his eyes. For almost an hour he counted the ticks of the clock and cursed the dawn's light streaming through the window. He went over a mental to-do list and added a call to the Dallas crime lab to request return of the evidence from the Durmorr murder. He stiffened like a stubborn mesquite tree—every inch of him—when he felt the mattress dip beside him.

Opening his eyes, he sent another glance at Val, discovering she'd turned over, her gaze trained on his face. "When did you get in?" she asked in a sexy morning voice.

"A while ago."

"Why didn't you wake me?"

Because that would have been a bad move. "I decided you needed your sleep, and so do I."

"Oh."

He hated the hint of insecurity in her voice and hated even more that he'd put it there. "I also knew that if I woke you, I'd want to take up where we left off last night. But since I realized I threw out my last condoms last week, I figured that probably wasn't a great idea."

She rose up on one bent elbow and supported her cheek with her palm. "Any particular reason why you threw out the condoms?"

"They were out of date." A really sad commentary on his life. "I plan to pick some up today as soon as the drugstore opens, unless you tell me we don't need them."

"Unfortunately we do need them. I'm not on any kind of birth control."

That figured. Against better judgment, he slid his arm beneath her and pulled her close to his side. "Now let's both try to get some sleep, although I'm not sure that I can. I'm pretty keyed up right now."

She snuggled closer to him. "Was it a bad wreck?"

The wreck was only one reason for his current state. Having

her so near was the other. "Yeah. A kid got in a hurry trying to make his curfew and took out a car. They both ended up in the culvert."

"They're okay, right?"

"They're alive, although the driver of the car was hurt pretty badly."

"How old is the boy?"

"Almost seventeen, and I've had trouble with him before. He has a souped-up truck and he's been caught speeding. He better hope the man he rammed is all right, otherwise he might be going to jail."

"The roads were slick. I'm sure he didn't intend to hurt anyone."

Valerie's defense of the kid surprised Gavin, although it probably shouldn't have. She had a lot of sympathy when it came to "crimes of necessity," something he'd learned last night. Something that had been bugging him, although he wasn't sure why. "Intended or not, he did hurt someone and he'll have to face the consequences."

She sighed. "I guess you're right."

They fell into silence for a long moment and Gavin thought she might be sleeping, until she asked, "Do you always wear your jeans to bed?"

He wore nothing to bed. Ever. "No."

"Then why do you have them on now?"

"Because if I take them off, then that means both of us will be in bed in our underwear."

"So? You can handle it. You're a tough guy."

"I'm still a guy."

"Okay. Suit yourself."

Val sat up and scooted toward the end of the bed, giving him another banner view of her butt. Before she crawled off the mattress, he reached up and clasped her arm. "Where are you going?"

She sent him a sour look. "To my bed so we can both get some sleep, at least for an hour or so."

"Look, Val, I've been cold all night long, and you're warm. I want you here."

She turned around, one leg dangling over the edge of the mattress. "Then I propose another option. You take off your jeans, climb under the covers and this time I'll stay behind you for a change. You shouldn't be uncomfortable because of me."

Hell, he'd still be uncomfortable without his pants. A nice kind of uncomfortable, if there was such a thing. Still, taking off his jeans wasn't the best option, because he wanted her wrapped soundly in his arms, close to his body. But if agreeing to that kept her in his bed, he'd deal with it. "Sounds like a plan."

"Fine." She worked her way back onto the bed and under the covers. "You can undress now."

Gavin slid off the bed onto his feet and turned his back on her as he skimmed off his jeans. He didn't want her to see his current predicament, otherwise she'd definitely leave. Still facing the wall, he stretched out on the bed beneath the covers, then reached behind and pulled her arms around him. He could feel the warmth of her breath between his bare shoulders. Worse, he felt the softness of her breasts pressed against his back. No way would he be able to sleep with her so close to him.

And to make matters worse, she patted his stomach right above his navel. "Are you okay now?" she asked.

"Not if you keep doing that." When she moved her hand to his chest, like some masochistic fool he slid it back down to his belly.

"You're too much," she said.

She was too much, Gavin decided, and she was also shaking— from laughter.

"You think this is funny?" he muttered.

"I'm sorry," she said, followed by another giggle.

In spite of the lack of wisdom, he rolled to face her. "I'm not sorry. I like to hear you laugh. You don't do it often enough."

Her expression went somber. "You're the first person in a long time who's given me a reason to laugh."

In another lapse of sanity, he slipped his leg between her bare thighs, bringing them as close as they could be with them both still dressed in their underwear. "Just call me the Good Humor man."

She ran her toes up and down the inside of his calf. "You're definitely a good man."

He pushed against her. "Want me to show you how good I can be?"

She frowned. "Either roll over or let me go to my bed before we get into trouble."

He lowered his mouth to within an inch of hers. "Just one little kiss first."

She frowned. "You don't know the meaning of a little kiss."

"Where you're concerned, that's definitely the truth."

Truth or not, Gavin kissed her anyway, deeply, urging a response from her. She also responded, when he slid his hand and palmed her breast beneath the shirt, with a soft sigh and a shift of her weight. Her response grew stronger when he slipped his hand down her belly, continuing beneath her panties to curl his hand between her thighs. Even if he couldn't have any relief right now, he could give her some. And that's exactly what he intended to do.

He worked her panties down, allowing him plenty of room to touch her, which he did without mercy, drawing a small sound from her mouth that was still firmly joined with his. He touched her lightly at first, then more insistently, until he had her exactly where he wanted her, opening up to him, lifting her hips toward him. Accepting him. Needing him. He broke their kiss to watch her face as he slid a finger inside her just in time to catch the pulse of her climax. Her eyes drifted close, her breasts rose and fell rapidly, her bottom lip trembled, and he wanted her with a fierceness he could barely contain.

Even though he took his hand away, he couldn't seem to completely break away from her. In fact, he moved partially over her, then completely on top of her because he didn't have the will to do anything else. He kissed her again as he fitted himself between her legs, moving his hips in a sorry imitation of the real thing. He wanted the real thing so badly that he physically ached. Valerie complicated matters when she raked her nails down his back and kept going beneath his briefs to massage his bare butt.

He broke the kiss to whisper, "I need to be inside you."

She moved her hands up to his back again. "You know we can't."

Never before had Gavin wanted to throw away all responsibility with a woman, but he'd never reacted so powerfully to anyone before Val, either. He lifted his head and looked into her hazy blue eyes. "Is this a bad time? I mean, could you get pregnant?"

"The worst time."

Clinging to the last of his faltering strength, he rolled onto his back, folded his arms behind his neck and stared at the ceiling. "I was afraid of that."

She shifted against his side again and laid her palm on his stomach. "I want to touch you," she said as she trailed a fingertip down the stream of hair below his navel, heading for hazardous territory.

He caught her hand and brought it to his lips, then turned his gaze to her. "I want to wait until we can do it right."

She looked offended. "What makes you think I can't do it right?"

"You know what I mean. When we can get there together."

"Okay." She rested both her head and her hand on his chest and sighed. "Tonight then."

He lifted her chin and brushed a kiss across her lips. "All night."

"For as long as it lasts."

As far as Gavin was concerned, that served as confirmation Val didn't plan to stay any longer than necessary. And that bothered him a lot. He was getting way too attached to her. Not a good thing, because she would eventually leave him, that much he knew. Unless he worked hard to convince her to stick around, maybe even continue to see him after she found her own place again, provided she didn't leave town. A tough job, but he was definitely up for the challenge.

"I'm going to take a shower now," he said as he got out of the bed before he changed his mind. Before he lost his mind.

"A long shower, I presume."

He turned at the door and caught her smiling, looking sleepy and sexy at the same time. "Nope. Just enough to cool me down a little."

"That's probably a good idea. Think I'll do the same."

When she stood, Gavin held up his hand. "If you join me, it's going to be all over but the moaning."

She folded her arms across her middle. "I meant take a shower in my bathroom."

"Oh." He shook his head and grinned. "Guess I just thought you couldn't stand to be without me for a minute."

She faked another frown. "Egomaniac."

"Now, darlin', you and I both know we can't stay away from each other for any length of time."

She took a step toward him. "So you say, lover boy."

He backed into the bathroom and closed the door partway, leaving the upper half of his body in the bedroom. "Come any closer, Val, and I'm not going to be responsible for anything I do to your person from this point forward."

She moved right in front of him, challenge in her eyes. "I'll see you tonight."

He reached out and pulled her mouth to his for another down-and-dirty kiss. "Maybe I'll see if I can clear my schedule and take a long lunch." Hell, all his friends were having nooners, why shouldn't he?

Val backed away and smiled. "I'll be here," she said, then turned and sent him a sassy look over her shoulder. "And don't forget the condoms."

That would definitely be the first order of business for the day, just as soon as he got out of the shower. In about an hour or so.

She was getting far too relaxed around him and making promises she shouldn't consider keeping. But Valerie couldn't seem to stop the strong feelings of anticipation, knowing that she would take Gavin as her lover tonight. She had set a course that she couldn't seem to stop. A course she didn't want to stop, regardless of the possible consequences.

All morning she'd been cleaning the house like a crazed

housekeeper on a tight schedule to alleviate her boredom and the ever-present guilt, even though Gavin had told her he had a woman who came and cleaned house once a month. She'd also needed to get her mind on something else other than the sheriff and what he'd done to her that morning. The activity hadn't helped a bit. He was never far away from her thoughts, and those thoughts continued to do things to her body that involved a lot of damp heat and deep longing. And to think they'd gotten so close this morning, well, that was just another example of her lack of control around him. Her lack of good judgment, too. But she wanted to be with him. Needed to be with him.

When she heard the phone ring, Valerie shut off the vacuum cleaner and rushed into the kitchen. Snatching up the receiver, she sucked in a breath before answering with a winded, "Hello," hoping upon hope to hear Gavin telling her he'd be home for lunch.

"Hey, Valerie, it's Manny."

Darn it. "Hi, Manny. What's up?"

"I know I said I'd give you a couple of days off, but I'm in a bind. Sheila's not feeling well today and Estelle has the flu. I need you to come in and help out with the Sunday lunch crowd."

Double darn. "You can't find anyone else?"

"Nope, and it's busier than a bull during mating season around here."

Valerie didn't appreciate hearing the word *mating* any more than she appreciated the abrupt end to her mini vacation. "Okay. I'll get dressed and get down there." Then she remembered her ailing car and the lack of keys to Gavin's vehicle. She'd handed them over last night and she hadn't seen them since. "You're going to have to send someone to get me. My car's still in the shop."

"I'll have Hal pick you up," he said, referring to the ancient part-time cook who came in to the diner when needed.

The man probably wasn't a day under eighty, and Val worried he handled his truck about as well as he handled the orders. "If that's the only option, guess I'll deal with it."

"Thanks, Valerie. I owe you for this."

"Yes, you do." She'd said it in a teasing tone, when in reality she was sorely disappointed. "See you later. Tell Hal I'll be waiting."

Exactly what she'd told Gavin that morning should he decide to come home at noon, before her boss's untimely request. Yet Manny had been nothing but kind to her, hiring her on the spot, never asking too many questions. He deserved her help when he needed it, and right now he did. Unfortunately she needed to be with Gavin in the worst way. At least they would have tonight.

Six

"**G**ot your message, so here I am."

When Gavin glanced up to see Connor Thorne walk through his office door, he gestured toward the chair in front of his desk. "Have a seat."

After he settled in, Connor asked, "What's up?"

Nothing good, Gavin decided. "I got a call from Mrs. Bradford, the widow who lives closest to Jonathan Devlin's house. She told me that she saw someone snooping around yesterday afternoon and she noticed some of the crime-scene tape was down this morning on her way to church."

"Did she recognize him?"

"Not him. Her. But that's all she could tell because she didn't have on her glasses. She went to get them, and the woman was gone when she returned."

"She didn't see a vehicle?"

"No, but I imagine she pulled around back."

"It's Gretchen."

Exactly what Gavin had decided when he'd received the report. "Yeah, and I'm wondering what she's looking for."

"Probably to see if she left anything that might implicate her in Devlin's murder," Connor said. "We found the syringes but the potassium was never recovered. Maybe it's in the house."

"But we've gone through the house thoroughly several times. If anything's there, we would have recovered it by now."

"Unless she's hidden it somewhere," Connor added. "The place is big and it's old with a lot of hiding places. We could have missed something."

Gavin leaned back and let go a rough sigh. "Could be, but I have a hard time believing it."

"Do you want me to take another look?"

"No, but I do have a favor to ask."

"Sure."

Gavin decided Connor might not be so enthusiastic after he heard him out. "I plan to stake out the place this evening for a while, maybe look around the outside and see if I can find something. If we're lucky, I might even catch Gretchen in the act. If we can hold her on breaking and entering, then we can gather enough evidence to charge her with Durmorr's murder. And we might have enough to compel her to give a DNA sample."

"Then you want me to go with you?" Connor asked.

"No, but I would like for you to take a second shift, maybe ten until midnight."

Connor forked a hand through his hair. "Nita's probably not going to like it."

Gavin didn't doubt that a bit. Connor's new wife had initially involved the Cattleman's Club when the first odd occurrences had started happening on Windcroft land. Even though they now suspected Durmorr had been digging up the property in search of the gold, they hadn't caught him at that time, but Nita Windcroft had definitely caught Connor. Not that Gavin believed for a minute Connor had played too hard to get. "Look, I'm running thin on deputies right now because this flu bug is rampant. I'd ask Logan, but he's got wedding plans to deal with, and Mark's bogged down with self-defense classes. Jake's playing mayor, and Tom and Rose aren't back from their honeymoon yet."

"So that basically leaves you and me to handle this," he said.

"Just for tonight. Two of my men should be back tomorrow, and that will help if I put a permanent patrol on the house."

Connor sighed. "I'll explain to Nita that the sooner we catch Durmorr's killer, the sooner this whole mess will be over and maybe we can put the Devlin-Windcroft feud to rest once and for all."

That damn feud had gone on too long, as far as Gavin was concerned. "I thought maybe that was calming down since Tom married Rose."

"It has, but it's been brewing for over a hundred years, so it's not logical to think it will go away in a few days."

Gavin wished the whole mess would go away, but that wouldn't happen until he put the killer away. And that would mean proving Gretchen Halifax was behind the whole thing. "I appreciate any help you can give me. I'd stay until midnight, but I have something pressing I need to do." Like finally making love with Valerie. And maybe that should make him feel guilty, but it didn't. If that didn't happen soon, he would continue to be distracted and do a half-assed job on the investigation.

"Did I say something funny?" he asked when Connor's grin widened.

"Just wondering if that pressing business has anything to do with a waitress residing in your house."

Figured. "You've been talking to Logan and Jake."

"The whole town's talking about it. You should know by now that nothing's sacred in Royal, especially when it comes to speculating on what happens between a man and a woman when the sun goes down."

If Gavin hurried, he wouldn't have to wait for sundown. "Well, they can talk all they want. I'm not saying anything other than she's a friend."

"A real good friend, I'm betting. In fact, we're all betting that—"

"I know about the bet, but I'm not giving any of you any satisfaction by revealing if or when anything happens between me and Val."

Connor looked more than a little doubtful. "I'll be damned. It's already happened, hasn't it?"

"No, it hasn't." That was the truth, for now but hopefully not for long. Gavin stood and offered his hand, feeling a strong urge to halt his friend's questions and get home for that long lunch. "Again, I appreciate this, Connor. Let's hope we can put this to rest by Christmas."

Connor pushed out of the chair and shook Gavin's hand. "Yeah, otherwise we may have a few wives and girlfriends ready to hang us all up to dry."

After Thorne left, Gavin picked up the phone to call Valerie and tell her he'd be home for a couple of hours—or three—just as soon as he stopped by the drugstore and bought a box of condoms. A big box.

The phone rang several times, and he assumed she was tied up or didn't feel comfortable answering. He could understand that.

Not a problem. He'd just surprise her. And he suspected she just might surprise him, too.

"I should've known I'd find you here."

Valerie nearly dropped the plate of country-fried steak in Lula Langford's lap before she slid it in front of the poor woman. "Here you go, hon. Enjoy."

She didn't give the woman any time to respond before she started toward the kitchen, Gavin following closely behind her. When she was safely behind the counter, she finally faced him. No matter how many times she'd seen him dressed in his sheriff's getup—cowboy hat, boots and jeans—he still took her breath.

"Manny needed me," she said after slipping the order pad into her apron.

He leaned over and gave her a dark, steamy look. "I needed you, too."

And she could say the same thing to him. "I know, but this couldn't be helped. Half the town's got a fever."

His smile arrived slowly. "I've got one, too. In fact, I'm burning up right now."

Val forced her gaze away from him and leveled it on the faded Formica counter. "Take two aspirin and go to bed, then."

"Not unless you're in bed with me."

She frowned. "Mind lowering your voice? Someone's going to hear you."

"Are you going to get off soon?"

He'd definitely walked right into that one, and she certainly wouldn't miss the chance for a premium comeback. "I would say that's entirely up to you, Sheriff."

He leaned a little closer. "One more comment like that, and I'm taking you back in the storeroom and having my way with you right here."

She shivered as if she was outside in the cold, not near the warmth of the kitchen at her back. "Give me a few minutes and you can take me home and have your way with me."

He pushed off the counter and his expression went serious. "Unfortunately I'm going to be tied up until ten."

Valerie checked the red clock on the wall. Now nearing 7:00 p.m., she would have to wait to have his attention for another three hours. "Tied up doing what?"

"I've got to do some surveillance at a crime scene."

"What about dinner?" What about their plans? she wanted to say. How selfish of her to think such a thing, but she couldn't help it. Right now she wanted to stomp her foot and whine like a petulant four-year-old.

"I can grab some coffee to tide me over," he said. "Right now food's the last thing on my mind."

From the heat in Gavin's dark eyes, Valerie knew what was on his mind. It was on hers, too. "I can come with you and keep you company."

"That means sitting in a vehicle basically staring at a house for a few hours. It's going to be cold."

"We can keep each other warm."

"Yeah, and that might keep me from doing my job."

"I'll behave myself."

He ran a slow finger down her forearm, now resting on the counter. "I'm not sure I will."

"I'll try not to distract you."

"That's not possible. But I guess I'll take my chances, as long as you can leave now."

Valerie untied and took off her apron, then tossed it under the counter. "I'm going, Manny," she called. "My ride's here."

Manny stuck his head through the opening of the kitchen. "Who's going to help clean up?"

She hurried to the coat tree and grabbed her jacket. "Hal can help you."

"Then I'll be here until midnight and…"

Valerie was out the exit before her boss could finish his protest and hurried inside the SUV. Once they were settled in, Gavin looked around, then leaned over and gave her a lingering kiss. He pulled back, but in a moment of weakness, Valerie grabbed his neck and tugged him back to her mouth. She wanted just a little more before he had to go back to being the sheriff. And later tonight she wanted all of him.

"Damn," Gavin said as he started the engine. "You're determined to make this little trip hard on me, aren't you?"

She smiled. "I don't know. Am I?"

He pulled out of the parking space and headed toward the outskirts of town. "Yeah, real hard."

"I'll try to be a good girl for the next few hours."

He reached over the console and took her hand to lay it on his thigh. "You better, otherwise I might have to drop you off at the house so I can do my job."

As he turned onto the road leading out of town, Valerie asked, "Exactly where are we going?"

"It's not too far from my place, relatively speaking."

That could mean miles, considering the expanse of land that sometimes divided Royal's rural homes. "Is it a ranch?"

"Not anymore. A few houses have been built around it, but at one time it was all by itself. It backs up to the Windcroft land.

You've probably heard a lot of talk about that place lately. Supposedly there's some gold buried there, although no one's ever found it."

"I've met Nita Windcroft." Valerie struggled to keep her tone even in light of the discovery. "She's married to Connor Thorne, right?"

"Yeah, and Connor's going to relieve me tonight."

Valerie found that very interesting. "Why Connor and not one of your deputies?"

"I'm understaffed at the moment," he said without further explanation, although Valerie suspected it had something to do with the semisecret society.

"The house we'll be watching belonged to Jonathan Devlin," he continued. "But it used to belong to Royal's notorious female outlaw, Jess Golden."

Valerie tried not to look too stunned, even though Gavin had inadvertently revealed another possible piece to the missing puzzle. Little did he know, he was assisting her in finding the answers she'd been seeking. And he was totally unaware he was doing exactly what she'd hoped he would do—lead her to the former home of her great-great-grandmother.

Considering what Gavin had seen in his lifetime, not much disturbed him anymore. But the historic house at the end of the pitted road had given him a bad feeling since the first time he'd seen it, even before its owner had been murdered. Of course, Jonathan Devlin hadn't met his death in the house itself, although that's where the process had begun. He'd been finished off in the hospital, with a final lethal dose of potassium chloride that would have gone undetected had it not been for his relatives' suspicions, spurred by a note Devlin had left with his will—a note that claimed he might be a target and nothing more. Now Durmorr, Devlin's killer, was dead, and Durmorr's murderer was still on the loose. And Gavin's gut told him that killer was Gretchen Halifax. Now if only he could prove it.

As he pulled into the drive and parked in the rear, Gavin noticed that Val seemed uncomfortable, too. "It looks more intimidating in the dark than it really is," he told her. "Wait here while I take a look around."

Gavin had his flashlight in hand and the door open, ready to exit, when Val laid her palm on his arm. "Can I go with you?" she asked, sounding apprehensive.

He considered the request for a moment, then decided he'd rather have her at his side instead of waiting alone in the SUV. "Sure. Just stay close to me."

"That won't be a problem at all," she said. "This place makes me nervous."

When they reached the end of the drive, Gavin lifted the yellow crime-scene tape, allowing Val to move beneath it before he took her elbow to guide her. He aimed his flashlight at the ground, looking for any signs of footprints belonging to an intruder. Nothing out of the ordinary so far, but they could have been covered up by the recent snowfall.

Gavin shone the beam along the house, searching for any obvious signs of finger or palm prints. After putting on a pair of latex gloves, he checked each window, finding one that rose with little effort. "The latch isn't holding on this one," he said. "Anyone with any kind of strength at all can get it open." Tomorrow he'd call someone to repair it. Of course, he doubted secure windows would stop anyone who had a mind to get in, namely Gretchen. No use making it easier on her, though.

"Who would want to get in there?" Valerie asked from behind him.

"My guess is whoever killed Malcolm Durmorr. They're looking for something in this house."

"What would that be?"

Gavin faced Valerie, keeping the flashlight aimed on the ground. "Since the investigation is ongoing, I'm not at liberty to say anything more. Some of the details of Durmorr's murder haven't been released to the public."

"I understand," she said. "Secrecy is part of the job."

"Yeah, it is." Although he couldn't see Val that well, he could tell that she was cold by the way she was huddled against the wall. "Let's go back to the truck and get you warm before you come down with pneumonia."

"I'm not a wimp."

He chuckled at her obstinate tone. "Believe me, I know that. But I'm about to freeze in my boots, so let's go."

Wrapping his arm around her waist, he held her close as he investigated the rest of the area with his flashlight. Back at the vehicle, he opened the door and gave her a quick kiss before helping her inside. He started the ignition to provide some heat until Connor could relieve him, but right now he could use a different kind of relief. All day long he'd thought about making love with Val, and having her there wasn't helping matters any, even though he wouldn't want her at home alone.

"Who owns the place now that Jonathan Devlin's dead?" Val asked after a time.

Gavin shifted in his seat to find her staring at the house. "The rest of the Devlin relatives. They can't settle the estate until we have this whole thing cleared up."

She glanced his way before turning her attention straight ahead again. "Does Connor Thorne live very far away?"

"Actually the Windcroft place is a couple of miles up the road. The boundary begins right beyond a small lake at the back of this property. The Devlins bought this place when it went up for auction, not long after Jess Golden skipped town and her mother moved away. The Windcrofts didn't like having a Devlin living that close to them."

"Why not?"

Gavin explained what he knew about the events that had taken place over a hundred years before, the accusations of cheating during a poker game when Richard Windcroft lost half of his land to Nicholas Devlin and then Devlin's murder not long after that being blamed on Windcroft.

"The feud had died down until Durmorr stirred it up again through a series of accidents at the Windcrofts'," he continued. "But we figure he was trying to cover what he was really doing."

"What was that?"

He decided it wouldn't hurt to tell her that much since the conjecture had made its way around town. "He was looking for the presumed buried treasure, the gold bars Jess Golden stole from Edgar Halifax, who was the mayor at the time."

That definitely got her attention, Gavin noticed. "Halifax?" she asked.

"Yeah, one of Gretchen's distant relatives. Anyway, when the map that supposedly indicates the exact location was found after Jonathan Devlin's death, the trouble started on the Windcroft land. A lot of holes dug around the place, accidents, that sort of thing. But it's a big area, so as far as we know, he didn't find it and we doubt he was working alone."

"And that means his partner in crime is probably the person who murdered him," she added for him.

"Could be."

When Valerie shivered and wrapped her arms tighter around her, Gavin reached into the backseat, retrieved a green plaid blanket and offered it to her. "Cover up with this. You'll be warmer, and I might be cooler."

She pulled the blanket up her chest. "Cooler?"

"Yeah. Your uniform's been distracting me since we've been in here. I don't understand why Manny doesn't let his help wear pants this time of year."

"He wants to keep the tradition going, unfortunately." Val leaned back against the passenger door and tucked the blanket beneath her thighs. "Any suspects in Durmorr's murder?"

He faked a scolding look. "Now, sweetheart, you know I can't tell you that."

She smiled. "There's nothing I can do to make you talk?"

"Oh, you can make me talk all right." He reached over and removed the band securing her ponytail, allowing her golden hair to fall to her shoulders. "But not about the case."

"Then what do you want to talk about while we're waiting?"

He draped his right arm around her shoulder, lifted the blanket and laid his left palm on her stocking-covered knee. "Maybe I don't want to talk at all."

She wagged a finger at him. "You're supposed to be keeping watch, remember?"

"I'd rather be watching you." And he would, the way he'd watched her last night before the damned interruption. The way he'd watched her this morning almost at his own peril.

"How long before the relief arrives?" she asked.

He slid his palm beneath her hem. "Not long at all, except these panty hose create a big problem."

She released a laugh, then a gasp when he curled his fingertips on the inside of her thigh. "I meant when is Connor supposed to be here to relieve you?"

Not soon enough, as far as Gavin was concerned. "In about an hour."

"And you really want him to happen upon us being naughty?"

Reluctantly he pulled his hand from beneath her skirt, deciding to save that until later. Still, he couldn't resist giving her a kiss. A quick, innocent kiss. But innocent wouldn't adequately describe what happened when he laid his lips against hers and she opened to him. Kissing Valerie was about as close to paradise as anything he'd ever experienced. Right now he would give up his duty to touch her, throw away all restraint to be inside her. The force of his need for her came out in a shudder that ran the length of him.

For his own sanity, he halted the kiss and tipped his forehead against her temple. "I want you so bad that I can't even think straight."

"I know what you mean. I haven't been thinking straight for the past few days."

He lifted his head and kissed her cheek. "I did remember to buy condoms."

Valerie gave him a self-conscious smile. "Actually I did, too. I walked to the little market down from the diner on my break. I went into the bathroom to gather my courage and then I realized I could actually get them from this machine hanging on the wall for a dollar. But I didn't have any quarters."

Gavin laughed. "Those multicolored specialty kinds?"

"Yes. I think they might actually glow in the dark."

"I bought standard-issue. Want to see them? They're in the backseat in a bag."

She toyed with his collar. "Something tells me we might not want to inspect condoms right now."

He slipped his hand below the blanket again and rested his arm beneath her breasts. "What else are we going to do for the next hour?"

"Are you suggesting we—"

"Make love right here? As much as I'd like to do that, it's not a good idea because we're in the company vehicle."

"But if we were in your car, that would—"

"Be kind of difficult but manageable."

She frowned. "You speak from experience, I take it."

"Not in that car. My dad wouldn't let me drive it when I actually went parking. But I did have a couple of nice trucks with a rear seat when I was in high school."

She tensed right before she lowered her eyes. "I see."

Gavin felt like a real jerk dredging up details that should be avoided. "Hey, that was a long time ago. Like I've said before, I don't believe in rehashing ancient history."

"It's not about your teenage antics, Gavin. It just reminded me of how differently we both grew up. I didn't own my first car until I was in college. Upper crust versus lower class."

He lifted her chin and turned her face toward his. "You have more class than most women I know. And how you lived in the past doesn't have any influence on how I see you as a person now."

"I hope so."

"I know so."

Gavin tried to convince her the only way he knew how, by kissing her again. He tried to keep it gentle, keep it light. Again Old Man Chemistry came bearing down on them both, encouraging them to hold each other tighter. He fondled her breasts through her uniform because his hands were still cold. She slid her hands up and down his chest, then over his stomach. When her palm came to rest on his thigh, that nearly sent him completely over the edge. At first he thought it might be inadvertent, but he soon realized she knew exactly what she was doing when she ran her fingertip along the ridge beneath his jeans.

He clasped her wrist and brought her palm to his lips for a kiss. "I'm not going to be able to last when I get you home if you keep going."

She collapsed against the seat and blew out a long breath. "I wish going home wasn't going to take so long."

Gavin decided it might not have to be that long. After snatching his cell phone from the holder attached to the dash, he dialed Connor's number, barely giving him the opportunity to say hello before he made his request. "I'm at Devlin's house and I know it's a lot to ask, but I need to get home a little earlier than I'd planned."

"Problems?" Thorne asked.

Yeah, a big one. He was on the verge of forgetting why he couldn't make love to Valerie right where she sat. "Just something I need to take care of. Not much going on here, so if you want to just drive by in a few minutes, maybe check out Gretchen's house, too, then you can go back to your wife."

"I can do that. I'll be there in about five minutes."

"Great. I owe you one."

When he hung up, Gavin turned to find Valerie looking at him with confusion in her expression. "Gretchen?" she said.

Damn. He hadn't meant to give that away. "She's reported a prowler a couple of times. She doesn't live too far from here." He hated to lie to Val, but this was a necessary lie.

"Are you going to wait until Connor shows up?" she asked.

No way, because Thorne might expect him to get out of the SUV. That might require a lot of explaining considering his current state. "He'll be here in a few minutes."

Gavin spun the tires in his haste as he backed out of the driveway. Turning onto the street, he saw approaching headlights and recognized the Windcroft logo on the side of the truck that passed, indicating relief had finally arrived—as least when it came to the job. The other kind was still foremost on his mind.

After they turned onto the main highway, Gavin punched the accelerator and flipped on the red-and-white lights, although he thought it best to forgo the siren. The lights usually required an emergency, but as far as he was concerned, this situation was an emergency.

They rode in silence, Val's head tipped against his shoulder, his hand on her leg beneath the blanket, hers wrapped around his arm. Every now and then he took his eyes from the road long enough to kiss her briefly. She slid her fingertips up and down his arm, and even through his down jacket he could feel every stroke, as though she was touching him somewhere a little lower. The tension was as thick as the snowdrifts lining the road, and through sheer will alone Gavin resisted the urge to pull over and forget the fact he was in an official vehicle.

As soon as they arrived in the drive, Gavin braked hard, grabbed the bag from the backseat and told her, "Let's go."

He rounded the hood and took Val's hand, practically dragging her up the walkway, until he cautioned himself to slow down. Now only a door, an alarm system and a short trip down the hall to his bedroom stood between him and his plans to make love to her all night. And if he didn't get the door open soon, he'd damn sure break it down.

Seven

The sound of the front door hitting the wall startled Valerie so much she actually gasped. Gavin muttered an apology when he kicked it closed, locked it and then swept her up into his arms. She'd never been carried away by a man, in either the literal or figurative sense, until she'd crossed over Gavin O'Neal's threshold. She'd never been totally robbed of breath from anticipation of what would happen next. And she'd never been so close to making what could be the biggest mistake of her life—losing herself to him completely before he knew the truth. But she would pretend to be the woman he believed her to be and carry this experience with her long after tonight.

Gavin opened his bedroom door with less force than when they'd come into the house and, once inside, flipped on the light and slid her down the length of his body. He simply stared at her for a long moment while she stood there clutching the front of his jacket. He removed her hands and kissed each palm, then left her to turn off the light, as if he sensed her self-consciousness. The part in the curtains provided some illumination, compliments of a three-quarter moon that made the snow look like blue glitter. The scene could be classic Rockwell, but the one now standing before her was definitely da Vinci. Gavin had removed his coat and shirt, revealing his body now cast in shadows—his work-of-art chest with the splash of hair in the center that traveled down the hard surface of his abdomen in a thin band.

Valerie inclined her head, studying all the details as if he happened to be on exhibit in a museum, not a bedroom. To think that she would soon have him closer to her than he'd ever been before, without any barriers, gave her cause to shiver, which she did.

Without speaking, he approached her slowly, pushed her coat off her shoulders and tossed it onto a nearby chair. She was very aware that the end of the bed was behind her where he backed her up, then turned her around and took his place in front of her. He dropped down on the edge of the mattress and pulled her between his parted legs.

"Take off your shoes," he told her, his voice impossibly deep.

Shoes seemed like a good place to start, so she used his shoulders for support as she toed out of her sneakers.

He reached up beneath her skirt and worked both her hose and her panties down her legs. After he dropped them on the floor, he slid his palms up her bare legs, then over her bottom. "We're going to take this slow," he said.

Val wasn't sure she wanted slow. Right then she craved fast and hard, but she could do nothing more than bend to his will, especially when he loosened the belt at her waist and released each button down the front of her dress. He worked the uniform off her shoulders, and once he'd completed that task, with one tug the dress dropped to the floor at her feet in a pool of polyester. Then he removed her bra without the least bit of hesitation.

Following a long visual once-over down her body, Gavin tugged her closer and placed an openmouthed kiss between her breasts before catching her gaze again. "You're so damn gorgeous, Val."

She smoothed her hands over his brown hair. "So are you."

"Come here." He brought her down on the bed beside him and kissed her again before coming to his feet.

Valerie recognized what was next on the agenda—Gavin O'Neal in all his glory. Her pulse picked up steam and so did her respiration when she considered the inevitable leap to complete intimacy was about to arrive. And she planned to actively participate in the sheriff's full disclosure.

"Let me," she said when his hand went to his fly.

"Gladly." Despite the darkness, she could see that he was smiling, could hear it in his voice. She so wanted to do this right, but her hands shook as she slipped open the button on his jeans. The zipper was even more problematic, and he laid his hand on hers to still it, allowing her to slide the tab down. Then he guided her palms to his waistband, urging her with his dark gaze as she pulled the denim down his narrow hips. He removed his briefs a little more quickly than any other clothing to this point—probably driven by impatience, Valerie decided. She was feeling a little bit impatient, too, her only explanation for the very bold, very precise visual exploration.

She might as well face it—he had it all. And he knew it, apparent when he just stood there and let her look her fill. But he wasn't exactly arrogant, just overtly confident. Every move he made shouted self-assurance, in his talk and unquestionably in his walk as he left her to rifle through the plastic sack, then approached the side of the bed and tossed several condoms on the nightstand. Definitely confident.

He centered his gaze on her while he turned down the bed, pulling the covers all the way to the end where she now sat, her arms folded across her bare breasts. He held out his hand and she took it without wavering, allowing him to haul her up into his arms, his bare flesh contacting hers.

With a gentle hand Gavin brushed her hair aside. "I have a couple of questions. First, are you still sure about this?"

So sure it scared her. "Yes."

"This isn't your first time, is it?"

Valerie could understand why he might think that, considering her nervous state. "No. But I've only been with—"

He halted her declaration with a quick kiss. "I don't need to know about your former lovers. In fact, I don't want to know about them."

Not that much to tell, Valerie thought. Only one other man whom she'd believed had loved her. A man who hadn't been able to accept her, despite the fact she had a college degree and a camaraderie with kids. A hard lesson learned about acceptance— or the lack thereof. As far as she was concerned, he no longer existed. Nothing existed except the desire in Gavin's dark eyes as he eased her onto the bed onto her back.

He took the place beside her, lifting up on one elbow to face her. "You have a great body, Val."

Funny, she'd always seen herself as more tomboy than temptress. Some had even described her as scrappy. Yet with the wave of a hand over her curves and the heat in his eyes, Gavin had somehow convinced her she was a voluptuous woman, deserving of his praise.

He bent his head to her breast and laved his tongue in slow circles around her nipple before drawing it into the warmth of his mouth. She closed her eyes, absorbed the wonderful sensations, her hands filtering through his hair. He paid close attention to her other breast, lingering there, sufficiently setting her senses on fire as he brushed his knuckles down her belly, then fitted his palm between her thighs. He knew how to touch her with a gentle caress that awakened long-neglected desire, just as he had that morning.

In a matter of moments she would leave reality behind and let undeniable need take over. As if Gavin sensed that, he took his hand away and reached toward the nightstand.

When he came back with the condom, Valerie discarded all her inhibitions and said, "I'll do it."

He handed her the condom and fell back onto the pillow. "Be my guest."

Valerie rolled to her side and touched him first, finally exploring him the way he had explored her. She heard the catch of his breath, felt a slight jerk of his hips and knew that he was as affected by her touch as she was by touching him. Although her hands slightly shook, she managed the condom without any real difficulty. Considering Gavin would soon be putting it to use made the simple process of thinking very difficult.

After nudging her onto her back, Gavin bent and parted her knees, then moved between them. Once again his hand idled over her flesh, sufficiently bringing her to the border of release. When he leaned forward, she expected him to slip into her gently. Instead he entered her with a hard thrust, then another, sending her completely into the grip of a powerful climax. She tipped her head back and experienced every pulsation that seemed timed with the beat of her heart.

Gavin stretched out on top of her, still joined to her body, and brought his warm lips to her ear. "Works every time."

Valerie wanted to scold him for his prideful tone, but she was too focused on his movements that had become much more tempered, at least for the time being.

He cradled her face in his palms and searched her eyes. "You feel incredible." Then he stopped moving altogether.

"What's wrong?" Valerie hated the note of panic in her voice, but she started imagining all sorts of things, the first of which was a broken condom. The second, he'd changed his mind.

His harsh sigh echoed in the silent room. "Nothing's wrong, and that's the problem. I've waited so long for you, and now it's almost too good. It's going to be over too soon."

"Gavin, it doesn't matter. We can always do it again in a while."

His sultry smile crept in. "Yeah, we sure can."

Apparently satisfied with that suggestion, Gavin moved in a steady rhythm while Valerie ran her palms down his back and on to the curve of his fantastic butt to experience each and every move of his hips. He drove harder, drove deeper, all the while keeping his gaze centered on hers. She saw a slight sheen of perspiration on his forehead, saw his determination to contain his passion. Then saw the transformation when he couldn't hold on any longer, when his eyes grew heavy-lidded and his jaw went taut.

His whole body tensed against her and he shuddered as his

eyes drifted closed. A long breath hissed out of his mouth, followed by a low groan and the sound of her name drifting from his lips before he collapsed against her.

Valerie listened to the sound of his ragged breathing, felt his heartbeat pound against her breasts as he laid his lips against her neck, cherishing every sweet moment. Having him so close felt so right, and again that brought on the remorse. She decided to push aside any negative thoughts to keep from destroying this little piece of paradise.

"It's all your fault, you know," he whispered after a time.

She framed his face in her palms and yanked his head up. "What's that supposed to mean?"

"You've been taunting me for months now, and that's why it didn't last any longer it did."

"I haven't been taunting you." She looked away. "Okay, maybe verbally taunting you, but that didn't have a thing to do with sex at the time."

"Maybe that's not how you meant it, but I've been up many a night thinking about us like this. I'm just glad we finally got to it and it turned out so well, even if it didn't last long enough."

Val kissed the cleft in his chin. "It turned out very well." When he started to shift away from her, she asked, "Where are you going?"

"I'm heavy, sweetheart. I need to move off you before I flatten you like a pancake."

For the first time in a long time Valerie experienced a total lightness of being and giddiness. "Nature's already taken care of that, Sheriff, so you don't have to leave on my account."

Grinning, Gavin palmed her breast, bringing Valerie's senses back to the forefront. "I've already told you—and I meant it—you have a great body. I like every inch of it."

And she liked having his hands on every inch of it. She started to tell him so, but her eyes began to water, her nose began to tickle and she turned away from Gavin to sneeze. "Sorry," she muttered, and Gavin followed with, "Bless you."

Then she sneezed again, two more times.

"Be right back." Gavin climbed out of the bed and headed into the bathroom, leaving Valerie feeling completely alone, and that was odd. She'd spent her life in cold, empty beds before she'd met him.

He came back after a time clutching a handful of tissues and offered them to her. "Here you go."

She took them and turned away to blow her nose, bringing about Gavin's laughter and Val's need to mutter another apology.

"I've seen you naked, Val. You can blow your nose in front of me."

She glanced over her shoulder to find him seated on the edge of the mattress. "That would be just plain rude."

He ran his fingers through her hair. "I hope you're not catching a cold after traipsing around in the snow tonight."

She rolled onto her back and grinned. "I always sneeze after sex and dusting."

He frowned. "Seriously?"

This time she laughed. "Not about the sex part. The dusting part, yes."

"Good. I'd hate to think you're allergic to me."

She wasn't, but she should be. "Do you want me to go back to my bed just in case I am catching a cold?"

He climbed back in beside her. "I want you to stay right where you are until we have to get up in the morning."

Valerie had never spent all night in bed with a man, but she had an inkling she was going to enjoy the experience with Gavin. "Okay, but I might be restless, especially if I keep sneezing." That seemed like a possibility considering her itchy nose. "And just in case—" she turned on the side away from him "—I'll stay over here."

He pulled the covers up over them, molded himself against her back and draped an arm over her waist. "You know something?"

She glanced back at him. "You're behind me again, and that usually spells trouble."

"Well, yeah, I am, but I was going to say you have an incredibly high body temperature. Kind of like having my own personal heater in the bed with me."

Val wriggled her bottom against him. She couldn't help it. "And it looks like I have my own personal thermometer."

Gavin nibbled on her ear. "And if you keep that up, it's going to be rising real soon."

She reached back and squeezed his bottom. "Now wouldn't that be a shame?"

"Yeah, a real shame." His hand drifted to her belly and below. "So let's see just how hot you really are...."

Gavin's skilled touch promised more pleasure for Valerie. Yes, she was going to like being in bed with the sheriff. A lot. But it was too much to ask to believe that she would be in his bed—or his life—for much longer.

The following morning Gavin awoke with empty arms and an empty space beside him. He sat up and looked out the window to see the first signs of dawn, but no Valerie. Most likely she was already up and about, getting ready for work, while all he could consider was getting his hands on her again. And again.

For a few minutes he entertained himself by staring at the ceiling. He couldn't quite peg why he didn't just roll over and go back to sleep for an hour or so. Okay, maybe he did know. Valerie Raines was keeping him up, in every way imaginable.

He liked having her in his bed beside him. He really liked being inside of her, something he'd discovered twice during the night. He could blame his overwhelming need for her on his recent span of celibacy, but sex was only part of the equation. He found everything about her fascinating, from the glimpses of her sense of humor to the way she always wrinkled her nose when she found something distasteful. He definitely liked her sharpshooter mind, as well as her killer body. Unquestionably her body. And one of these days he planned to break through that invisible shield she used to guard her emotions. Right now he planned to find her.

First stop—the guest room. But when Gavin found the bed empty and still made, he walked to the bathroom door and knocked lightly. "Val, are you in there?"

When she didn't answer, he headed for the kitchen. She could be making coffee or breakfast, but he didn't detect any of the usual cooking smells. As he bypassed the great room, he saw something from the corner of his eye and stopped short.

There she was, curled up on the sofa, wrapped in a throw, with only her head exposed. Right away he noticed her pale skin, the glaze of perspiration on her forehead and the fact that she was shaking beneath the blanket.

Concern sent him straight to the couch and down beside her. He laid a hand on her forehead and his worry increased. "You're burning up."

"I'm freezing," she said between chattering teeth. "I hope you don't mind but I turned up the heat."

"You need to go back to bed."

She barked out a cough and stared at him with dull eyes. "I promised Manny I'd work today. I have to go in for the breakfast crowd."

Gavin sent her a hard look. "You have the flu and you're not going anywhere."

Not waiting for further protests, he scooped Val into his arms, walked down the hallway and deposited her back in his bed. Strangely enough, she didn't argue, but considering how ill she looked, he figured she was probably too weak. "Don't get out of this bed. I'll be right back. I need to make a phone call."

At times like these, Gavin wished he could call his mother. She'd been good at taking care of him when he'd been sick as a child and she would know what to do. But she was gone, had been for a long time, so he'd have to call someone else who could give him solid advice.

He strode to his office, pulled the key from the hiding place beneath the desk and unlocked the drawer. A good two minutes had passed before he finally found the directory listing all present and former members of the Cattleman's Club. He knew one doctor fairly well, and although the guy was a plastic surgeon, he would be able to help—or at least Gavin hoped so.

He pounded out Justin Webb's private number and waited for

what seemed like hours for an answer. Before the man barely got out the word *hello,* Gavin started in. "This is O'Neal, Doc. Sorry to bother you, but I need a favor. I know this isn't your thing exactly, but I have a friend who's sick. She's got a fever and she looks awful and—"

"Slow down, Sheriff," Justin said. "She's probably got the flu. Half of the hospital's been out with it. Not much you can do but let it run its course."

That wasn't good enough for Gavin. "What about medicine?"

"Do you have some kind of pain relievers?"

"Yeah, some aspirin." And hopefully it hadn't expired like the box of condoms.

"Just give her that to keep the fever down and over-the-counter cold remedies for any kind of cough. Make sure she gets plenty of fluids so she doesn't dehydrate. Other than that, watch her. If she gets any worse, call me and I'll have one of my colleagues see her. Or bring her into the E.R."

If that was the best the doc could do, Gavin guessed he'd have to live with it. "Thanks, Justin. I appreciate your help."

"Not a problem. Is this someone special? Maybe a waitress from down at the diner?"

He'd be damned if the grapevine hadn't already crawled across the entire city and crept into the hospital. "Yeah, that's her." And she *was* special. More special than anyone could know. But he knew, and that's all that mattered at the moment.

"Good luck, Gavin. I hope you don't get this stuff. It's bad."

"Thanks again, Justin," he said and hung up.

Gavin could normally handle "bad" in most situations, including delivering bad news to families of crime victims. But he'd never had to deal with taking care of someone sick. Not an issue at the moment. He planned to take care of Val for as long as it took for this bug to pass. Maybe even longer, if she would let him.

On that thought, he dialed his best deputy's number, Annie Rivera, the lone female on the force. She wasn't much bigger than Val, but she was tough as a barbwire fence and could handle any grief the rest of the guys tossed at her. "Rivera," he said when she answered. "I need you to take over for me for a few days."

"What's wrong, Sheriff?" She sounded almost alarmed, and rightfully so. He hadn't missed a day of work since he'd signed on with the department, even before he'd taken over as sheriff.

Gavin faked a cough. "I've got the flu and I feel like hell."

"I'm not surprised," she said. "It's definitely going around. What do you want me to tell Opal Devlin about the murder investigation?"

He didn't have the energy to deal with Durmorr's aunt. "You've talked to her?"

"Yeah, late yesterday. I'm not sure she's as concerned about finding her nephew's killer as she is about finding out when the house will no longer be designated a crime scene. She wants to sell it as soon as possible."

"Tell her she'll be the first to know when the house is cleared." A lie. Tom Devlin would be the first to know since he was helping with the investigation.

"Okay, Sheriff," Annie said. "Take care. I can handle it in your absence. Don't rush back too soon."

He didn't plan to do that until he was assured Valerie was well.

After he hung up, Gavin strode into the kitchen and found aspirin that was fortunately still good. He grabbed up the bottle, retrieved a glass of water and went back to Valerie. She was facing the door, covered up to her chin, her eyes closed and her face flushed from the fever.

Gavin experienced a fierce surge of protectiveness that weighted his chest. He needed to make her better even though he had very little to offer her but a couple of pills and his undivided attention. Crossing the room, he sat on the bed and brushed the hair away from her damp forehead. Her eyes drifted open and she attempted a weak smile. "Can you sit up for a minute?" he asked.

"Sure." She scooted up slowly, her back resting against the headboard.

"Take these." He opened her hand and placed the pills in her palm. "They'll help with your fever."

She put the pills in her mouth, took a swallow of the water, then moved back down on the bed. "Thanks."

Gavin set the glass on the nightstand, stood and pulled a chair next to the bed beside her. "Now you need to rest. I'm right here if you need anything."

She managed a frown. "You don't have to babysit me, Gavin. You go on to work. I'll be fine."

He shook his head. "No way. I'm not leaving you alone. The department will get by without me today." And tomorrow and the next day, if need be.

She lifted her hand and laid it on his arm. "I appreciate it, but—"

"No more arguments," he said as he grabbed up the TV remote from the nightstand. "Anything in particular you want to watch?"

She yawned. "I think I'll just sleep for a while."

Real stupid, O'Neal. Of course she'd want to sleep. She was sick, and he was not very good at this. "Sure." He snapped off the TV and settled back in the chair.

"You can watch TV," she said. "It won't bother me."

Her continuous shaking bothered Gavin. A lot. "Don't worry about me. Just close your eyes."

"I only want a little nap," she said. "I'll be okay in a while."

Gavin kept his gaze focused on the blank TV screen, but when he realized she was asleep, he kept watch on her like a sentry guarding precious cargo. He supposed that when you cared about someone, this was a part of the deal. That whole "in sickness and in health" thing.

Whoa. He was getting way ahead of himself. He still had a lot to learn about Val before he even considered anything close to vows. Yet he recognized she moved him in ways he'd never been moved before. How could he not? She was tough on the outside, had a soul-deep compassion, yet at times she seemed almost insecure. Not that she'd meant to reveal that to him, but he'd seen it. And he wanted to prove to her that she was a beautiful woman, however long it took.

No denying it. Val had affected him more than any woman he'd been involved with to that point. Maybe that should send him running scared, but he didn't feel like running. He didn't plan to go anywhere and he didn't want her to leave either.

Tucking those thoughts away for the time being, he rested his head against the chair, laced his hands together on his belly and closed his eyes. He could definitely use some sleep, too.

The sound of Val's moans jerked Gavin out of his short-term nap and the chair. He stood over the bed, watching her thrash, her expression reflecting what appeared to be pain and a good deal of distress.

He shook her arm gently. "You're okay, sweetheart. I'm right here."

"You're hurting me," she said without opening her eyes, causing Gavin to release his grasp on her.

"Val, it's just a dream. It's the fever."

"You don't understand," she whispered. "I had to do it. I *had* to."

Finally she settled down and turned away from him. Gavin decided the illness had her talking crazy. Still, the content of her ramblings disturbed him.

As he settled back into the chair, he couldn't help but wonder who exactly had hurt her and what exactly she had done.

Eight

Random images from her past floated in and out of Valerie's fuzzy brain. Images of transgressions she couldn't take back, mistakes she had made. Pain. Humiliation. Fear.

The handcuffs hurt her wrists. The sirens hurt her ears. She wanted out of the car. She couldn't breathe. She felt sick.

Then she felt her grandmother's careworn hands reaching out to her, soothing her fevered forehead.

"I'm here, Val. It's okay."

She came awake with a start, realizing she hadn't heard her grandmother's voice at all. The timbre was too deep, too male. For a moment she remained disoriented to time or place, until she saw him sitting by the bed. Gavin O'Neal, her beloved savior.

Valerie pushed her hair out of her face and considered sitting up, but she felt too weak to attempt even that simple maneuver. She craved liquid for her parched throat and her sandpaper mouth. "Water." Her voice sounded raspy, more like a croak.

Gavin offered her a glass with a straw. "Here. It's lemon-lime soda. Hope that's okay."

"It's fine." She couldn't really taste anything anyway, but the soda helped her thirst, and that was all she cared about at the moment. After a few sips, she dropped back onto the pillow. "What time is it?"

"After 9:00 p.m. You've been in and out all day long."

In and out of fitful dreams, Valerie thought. "I can't believe I've slept that long."

"You needed your sleep. Is there anything else you need right now?" he asked, both his tone and his expression reflecting his concern.

She coughed and swiped at her watery eyes. "Yes. A hot shower."

"How about a hot bath?"

Valerie couldn't think of anything more inviting than soaking in a whirlpool, except maybe the sheriff's smile. "That sounds good."

Gavin came to his feet. "I'll just go get you some clean clothes and be back in a second."

"No!" Valerie cringed at her harsh tone. "I mean, I can do that myself."

He laughed. "I promise I'm not going to check out all your underwear. Besides, you've already shown them to me."

Gavin perusing her underwear wasn't Valerie's major concern. What he might find beneath that underwear was. She sat up and draped her legs over the edge of the bed. "I promise I can handle getting my own clothes."

"Are you sure? You've got to be fairly weak since you haven't eaten all day, on top of the fever."

She stood on shaky legs. "I'm okay. It's only a short trip."

"Okay, if you're sure." He pointed toward the bathroom. "I'll go start the water running. Holler if you need me."

She lifted one leaden arm and patted his cheek. "I will."

When she walked into the hall, the first wave of nausea attacked her empty stomach. She drew in several deep breaths and leaned against the wall until it passed. Although her room was next to Gavin's, it seemed as if it were blocks away. By the time she reached the bureau, she had to sit on the bed for a few moments before she had the energy to retrieve her panties and a thin cotton gown, the only thing clean at the moment since she hadn't done any laundry. She sat a while longer before making the journey back into Gavin's bedroom.

Valerie found him waiting at the bathroom door sporting a huge towel and a frown. "You look pale, Val." He caught her arm just as she began to sway. "Are you sure you're up for this?"

No, she wasn't, but she could at least try. "I'm sure."

He took her elbow and guided her into the bathroom, set her down on one of the steps leading to the whirlpool and reached behind her to turn off the water. Then he took her hands and pulled her up. "Just lean on me," he said as he started to slip the buttons on her shirt.

She loosely clasped his wrist as a fiery blush climbed up her throat. "I'm not completely helpless."

He tugged her hand away. "But you are sick. Besides, it's nothing I haven't seen before." He grinned. "And I promise not to look."

Smiling back took a lot of effort on Valerie's part, but she didn't mind. "Right now I'm too drained to argue with you."

He had her shirt off with the expediency of a man who'd had a lot of practice. "Hang on to my shoulders," he told her as he removed her bottoms.

Now she stood before him naked and shivering, her arms crossed over her bare breasts. But he didn't hesitate before he turned her around and helped her up the steps. He didn't let her go until he had her settled into the swirling water.

Valerie expected him to leave her, but instead he settled onto the wide edge of the tub, his long legs bent at the knees, his sock-covered feet resting on the top step. "Is the water okay?" he asked.

"It's perfect." She lifted her hair and laid her head back against the towel he'd draped over the end and scooped up a handful of foam into her palm. "Do you take a lot of bubble baths?"

He shook his head. "No. One of the guys gave me the stuff for my birthday as a joke. In fact, I've never even used this tub before."

"I'm surprised. Looks big enough to host a party."

"Nope. No parties in the tub."

Valerie closed her eyes and released a soft sigh. "This is the next best thing to a party. You should try it."

"Maybe I will, when you're better and we can do it together."

Even though Valerie felt as if she'd slammed into a brick wall running full force, she couldn't help but entertain a few images of bathing with Gavin. Now she knew she was sick—in the head. "Sounds nice."

The next thing Valerie knew, she felt the glide of fingertips through her hair. She looked up to find Gavin standing behind the platform and she hadn't even realized he'd moved. She closed her eyes again as he began to massage her temples, all her cares seeming to drift away with every gentle caress. "You're spoiling me," she managed, followed by another satisfied sigh.

"Good. You deserve to be spoiled."

Valerie deserved to be horsewhipped considering what she had been keeping from him. "I probably should wash up now before I turn into a prune."

He tipped her face up and kissed her forehead. "I'd offer to help you do that, but I'm not that strong."

Neither was she, even if she was sick. "Okay. I'll be out in a bit."

"Stay right where you are. I'll be back to help you out in a few minutes."

"Gavin, I can—"

"Fall and hit your head. Then you're going to be a lot worse off than you are now."

He rounded the tub, walked to the door and pointed at her. "I mean it, Val. I'll be gone ten minutes tops. And you better still be in that tub when I get back."

She sent him a lazy salute and even that took a lot of exertion. "Okay, Sheriff."

After giving her a soft smile, Gavin walked out, leaving Valerie alone to bathe. She raised her head and looked around. How sad was this whole scene? She was in a gorgeous guy's whirlpool, naked and alone. No wine waiting for her in the bedroom, just a glass of flat soda. No soft music playing in the background, just the sound of her rapid-fire sneezing. She had weepy eyes and a pachyderm residing on her chest. No doubt her nose was red and her hair probably looked like the backside of a briar patch. Yet Gavin hadn't seemed to notice. He'd only been kind and considerate, tending to her needs as if he truly cared about her well-being. As if he was responsible for making her better.

Feeling misty and miserable, Valerie concentrated on cleaning up for fear she might actually have an emotional meltdown. Only the flu, she told herself as she grabbed the rag and a bar of soap that smelled like Gavin. The sense of utter helplessness, the fever, had shoved her down in the dumps. Having a bath would help, even though the simple act of washing sapped her of strength. Tomorrow she would feel better. She had to.

Gavin came back into the room looking totally charming with his unshaven face and his tattered jeans and T-shirt. After setting aside the towel, he approached the tub, hands tucked away in his pockets. "Are you about finished?"

Valerie sat up and swiped the tendrils of wayward hair from her forehead. "Sure."

He took her arm and helped her stand, then wrapped her in the terry bath sheet, all the while averting his gaze. He assisted her down the stairs and guided her to the vanity, where he held up a black flannel nightshirt dotted with red hearts. "I thought you might be more comfortable in this."

She pointed to the cotton gown resting on the vanity. "I already have something to wear."

"It's too skimpy. You need something warmer."

She braced one hand on the white granite counter for support and studied the shirt. "Where did you get that?"

He shrugged. "It was another gift, and not one that I appreciated."

Valerie should leave it at that, but curiosity commandeered her good sense. "From a girlfriend, I take it."

"From a former acquaintance," he said, with heavy emphasis on *former*. "Now let's get you dried off."

Gavin tugged the towel away and patted her down, again keeping his gaze away from her body. He had her dressed in his nightshirt and her panties faster than she'd ever thought feasible, achieving the task without really looking at her. She'd never dreamed she would ever encounter a man willing to treat her with such care and respect.

He wrapped his arm around her waist and said, "Back to bed."

Valerie leaned heavily on him as he led her to the bed and pulled back the covers for her to climb in. After he had her settled, he told her, "I'll be right back."

He was gone for a few minutes before returning with a lap tray containing a bowl and another glass of soda. After setting it aside on the nightstand, he propped the pillows against the headboard. "Scoot up."

She wrinkled her nose when he placed the tray in her lap. "I'm not hungry."

He sat on the edge of the bed and laid a napkin across her chest. "Sheila brought this soup by just for you after Manny told her you were sick. She claims it's a cure-all."

Valerie leaned her head back against the pillow and groaned. "Manny. I forgot all about calling him."

"Not a problem because I did it for you."

"Is he mad at me?"

"He wasn't happy, but I assured him you were in no shape to work and that he wouldn't want you infecting all his customers. I also called the garage about your car. They said they're backed up, but they promised to have it ready by early next week. Rhodes told me he'd work on Sunday if he had to."

Next week? "Great. I was hoping it would be ready in the next couple of days."

"You probably won't be well enough to drive it in the next couple of days." He held the spoon to her lips. "Now try a bite of this."

She took a sip of the warm liquid that tasted like salty nothing. "Are you happy now?"

"Not until you have a little more."

Reluctantly she accepted a few more spoonfuls before she nudged his hand away. "Enough. My stomach is starting to protest."

"Fine." He took the tray away and offered her the soda. "Have a little of this. The doc said you need plenty of fluids."

She took a quick sip and laid her head back on the pillow. "You called a doctor?"

Gavin set the glass aside. "Yeah, while you were asleep. I was worried."

He looked worried, and Valerie needed to tell him how much his concern meant to her. "Thank you. I appreciate everything you've done for me."

"Not a problem." He grabbed up the TV's remote control. "Now move over and let's see what's happening in the world."

She gladly complied, edging aside to allow him room. He settled beside her and turned on the TV to Melissa Mason reporting the local news. "She's an excellent anchor," Valerie said. "Very pretty, too."

"Yeah, but I'm surprised she's working. She's about to marry my best friend on Saturday." He tugged Valerie to his side and leaned his head against hers. "And if you're feeling up to it, you can go with me."

Valerie could think of many reasons why that wouldn't be a great idea. "I won't know anyone, Gavin."

"Sure you will. You've probably met all the guests at one time or the other down at the diner."

"I don't have anything appropriate to wear." And that was the truth.

"It's going to be a small ceremony at Logan's house next door. Nothing elaborate. We'll just see how it goes between now and then."

Valerie started to bring out more arguments until she realized Gavin had turned his complete attention to the television, where Melissa was saying, "According to a spokesperson from the sheriff's department, there have been no new leads in the Malcolm Durmorr murder investigation...."

Gavin hissed a rough sigh and snapped off the TV. "Like I don't already know that."

Valerie stared up at him. "And I'm keeping you from doing your job."

He gave her a gentle squeeze. "I've got other people working for me. They can handle it until you're better. And in order for you to get better, you need to sleep."

"Maybe I should go back to my room. Otherwise, you might catch this bug."

He rolled to his side to face her, jaw propped on his palm. "I'm fairly sure I've already been exposed. And I want to be here with you in case you need me."

The sincerity in his voice, in his expression, caused an annoying lump to form in Valerie's throat. Tears she'd been so determined not to shed filled her eyes. Unwelcome tears that she'd always been able to control, kept tucked away after she'd learned all too well that crying never got a person anywhere.

Gavin reached back for a tissue and dabbed at her damp cheeks. "Hey, sweetheart, it's going to be okay. You'll be better before you know it."

"I know, and it's just that…" She released a rogue sob. "It's just that…"

"What?"

"No one's ever really cared for me like this before other than my grandmother. Your willingness to do this for me, well, it amazes me." And touched her so deeply she sensed another fresh rush of tears coming on.

He brushed a kiss across her cheek. "To tell the truth, Val, I've never taken care of anyone before. So if I'm doing anything wrong, you're just going to have to let me know and be patient with me."

Problem was, Gavin had done everything right, and that made Valerie want to go into a full-fledged crying jag. "You're doing wonderfully."

"And you need sleep," he said. "Now blow your nose and I'll turn out the light."

After he sent the room into darkness, he slid his arm beneath her and held her close. Valerie laid her head on his chest, counting the beats of his heart against her ear. A strong heart. A good heart. A good man. The best. At that moment she wanted to stay with him indefinitely, more than she'd ever wanted anything in her life. More than she wanted to discard the ever-present shame. More than she wanted to find the treasure and resolve the remnants of her past.

But these precious nights in Gavin's arms would only be a temporary respite from the truth. Once he knew that truth, he might never want to see her again, much less touch her. Right now she had to get some sleep and get well. Tomorrow she would be better.

When Val got worse before she got better, Gavin O'Neal learned a lot about himself. In four days' time he'd learned he could sleep with a woman with the sole purpose of sleeping—when he wasn't watching her well into the night, listening to her breathing, touching her forehead to make sure her temperature hadn't risen. He'd learned he could bathe her body without any serious thoughts of sex. He'd learned how to prepare chicken soup and how to totally tune out the work that was piling up while he gave her his complete attention. He hadn't realized his capacity for worrying so fiercely over someone or that he could celebrate something as simple as a fever finally breaking.

He'd also begun to understand what a tough time she'd had growing up, even though she was still guarded about her past. He'd learned the depth of her selflessness when she claimed that she'd known others who'd been worse off than she had been and the strength of her compassion when she'd told him about the troubled kids she'd worked with while in college. Above all, he'd come to realize she was a very special lady, and because of that his feelings for her had grown deeper with every moment he'd spent in her presence.

At first he'd tried to liken it to being in the trenches in a less-than-favorable situation, the way he had been with various partners during his law-enforcement career. But this was more. A hell of a lot more. He hadn't wanted to be that close with any of his colleagues and he never had been. Not once had he ever discussed his parents' murders with any of them or his overriding grief that still visited him even after all this time. Yet he'd been that open with Val on more than one occasion, and she'd seemed to genuinely understand.

Yeah, she was special all right, as well as stubborn. That much Gavin had discovered that morning when she'd insisted on going back to work, since it was Saturday, and he hadn't been able to stop her. He'd taken the opportunity to go into the department, even though he only spent a couple of hours shifting papers on his desk before he ran a few errands. He had a wedding to attend and a few plans to make, so he'd cut out early with the excuse that he still felt poorly even though he hadn't had a sniffle.

Now nearing 5:00 p.m., he was heading home in hopes that Val had lived up to her promise only to work through lunch. When he pulled up in the drive, he found the GTO parked in the garage, indicating she had returned. A good thing, he decided. He could give her the first of several surprises he had planned for their evening.

With a sack gripped in his hand and a bag draped over his arm, Gavin tore into the house like a kid seeking praise for a good report card. He called to Valerie and when he didn't get an immediate response, a host of concerns followed him all the way down the hall to his room. What if she'd overdone it and passed out? What if she'd fallen and hit her head with no way to get to the phone? What if someone had broken into the house…? No. He wasn't even going to go there.

Once in his bedroom, he tossed the sack on the bed and laid the clear bag beside it, then headed straight for the bathroom, only to find it deserted. He paused a minute to push the paranoia away. Most likely she was in the guest room, changing out of her work clothes. If that proved not to be the case, then he'd keep searching until he found her, even if that entailed scouring every inch of his acreage and every square mile of the county.

The minute he hit the hallway, Gavin heard the buzz of a hair dryer coming from behind the guest room's partially closed door. Relief immediately settled over him, but for some unknown reason he had to be sure. He walked through the door and continued on to the bathroom, where he found Val standing in front of the vanity, bent at the waist, dryer in hand, finger-combing her hair as the strong flow of air blew it in all directions. Only then did he realize she was wearing a shirt that hit her midthigh. His shirt, and apparently not much else.

Gavin really liked seeing her in his clothes. In fact, he liked everything about her, especially her legs. Well-toned legs but not so muscular that they didn't look feminine. He was assaulted by the image of going to his knees before her and running his hands up her bare thighs—and higher. Before he could act on that urge, she snapped off the dryer, set it on the vanity and pushed her hair out of her face.

She gasped when she caught sight of him in the mirror's reflection and spun around, hand at her throat. "You startled me."

He stayed propped against the door frame, otherwise he might tackle her where she stood. He'd already given her one jolt, she didn't need another. "Sorry. I just got home and I couldn't find you. I thought maybe you'd left town without telling me."

She grabbed a brush and ran it through her tangled locks. "I wouldn't do that."

Gavin liked to think she wouldn't desert him without a goodbye, but he got the feeling that one day he'd come home to find her gone. "You look good in my shirt."

Val stopped brushing her hair and looked down as though she'd forgotten what she was wearing. "I think it makes a nice fashion statement." After tossing the brush aside, she hoisted herself up on the vanity and smiled. "Actually I got so used to having you around, I really missed you today. And since I didn't know when you'd be home, I decided to keep something of yours close to me. Kind of corny, huh?"

Gavin decided it was the sweetest thing he'd ever heard. He crossed the room and stood before her, itching to touch her, to take that shirt off her slender shoulders and kiss her all over. "I don't mind you wearing my clothes, as long as you don't expect me to wear yours."

She slapped playfully at his chest. "Like you could actually fit into them."

"True." He shifted one random strand of hair away from her cheek. "How are you feeling?"

She sent him a coy look, took his hand and laid it on her bare thigh. "Why don't you see for yourself?"

Man, oh, man, did he want to. Unfortunately time was scarce. If he didn't control himself now, he wouldn't be able to later. "Well, sweetheart, that sounds like a plan, but I have to get a shower and get over to Logan's house in about forty-five minutes. I'm the best man."

Val draped her arms around his neck and wet her lips. "I'm sure you are the best man, but I wouldn't object to you providing more proof."

Neither would Gavin, but responsibility to his friend prevented him from doing what he wanted to do with her. To her. "Tell you what. We can definitely take that up later tonight, after the wedding."

She sighed. "I guess I can wait." She hopped down from the counter and landed right up against him. "Why, Sheriff, I do believe your body's having a complete uprising."

Despite caution clawing at his brain, he circled his arms around her. "Now what gave you that idea?"

Val had the nerve to wriggle her hips. "As you've informed me previously, you don't carry your weapon in your pants. Although I could say you're definitely armed right now."

He lowered his mouth and flicked her earlobe with his tongue before meeting her gaze again. "And if you keep rubbing against me, I could get trigger-happy real fast."

She slid her hands up and down his back. "But you don't have time right now."

"Unfortunately no." Dammit.

Her lips curled into a smile. "You big tease."

"I could say the same about you."

"Believe me, Gavin, I'm not teasing."

He could tell she wasn't teasing. Not in the least. But she was damn sure tempting him to forget about his duties. "Either we stop right now or you're going to have to explain to the groom why I'm late for his nuptials."

She sidestepped away from him, her arms folded beneath her breasts. "Okay. I'll be here when you get back."

"You're going with me."

"I told you, I don't have anything to wear."

"Yeah, you do." Taking her hand, Gavin hauled Val into the bedroom, guided her to the bed and indicated the dress. "This is for you."

She lifted the plastic covering and ran her palm over the silky red fabric. "Oh, my gosh. You picked this out all by yourself?"

"I had a little help from friends." More accurately a friend's wife.

She just stood there staring at it, leading Gavin to believe that maybe he hadn't made the correct choice. "You don't like it, do you?" The insecurity in his tone surprised Gavin because that wasn't his normal behavior. But then, he'd surprised himself on many levels lately, thanks to Ms. Raines.

Valerie faced him, genuine appreciation in her eyes, as though he'd handed her the moon and stars in one helping. "It's absolutely beautiful."

He swiped away an unexpected tear trailing down her cheek. "Hey, it's only a dress, sweetheart. No big deal."

She laid her palm on his hand where it framed her face. "It is to someone who's never had a dress like this before."

To think that Val had done without so many things in her lifetime caused a heavy weight to land on Gavin's heart. Taking her into his arms, he stroked her back, held her close and realized that she meant more to him than he'd ever thought possible. She made him feel things he'd never felt before, want things he'd never before wanted. He'd walk through fire to make her happy. He'd do anything to show her she was safe with him and wanted. Later tonight he planned to tell her that very thing.

Regrettably right now he had to get a move on, otherwise he would be late. Pulling away, he pressed a kiss on her lips and said, "The bag has a pair of those really sexy stockings in it, the kind that have the lace at the thighs. And some shoes. The saleslady guessed at your size, but then she said she's been in the diner and she's seen your feet."

Val smiled. "Must be Mrs. Briggs. She's always looking at everyone's feet."

"As weird as that sounds, it's probably a good thing. I wouldn't begin to know your size."

She stared down at his boots. "I'd bet that you wear a size twelve."

Now how had she known that? "Damn, you're good."

She let go a laugh. "Actually I looked in your closet, so I cheated a little. I wanted to know if that whole thing about a man's feet—"

He placed his palm over her mouth. "Don't go there, Val. Not unless you want me to be ostracized for months for being tardy."

After pulling his hand away, she tapped a finger against her lips. "I'll let you go as soon as you kiss me like you mean it."

Not a problem, Gavin thought. He did mean it, and when he told her tonight exactly how he felt about her, he'd mean it then, too. More than she could ever know.

Nine

If someone had told Valerie two weeks ago that she would be witnessing the wedding of Gavin O'Neal's best friend, she would have called the person a lunatic. But then, if anyone had claimed she would be staying with the sexy sheriff—*making love* with the sheriff—she would have doubled over with laughter.

Yet here she was, in the home belonging to rancher Logan Voss, waiting for the ceremony to begin. Valerie recognized most of the small group of guests from the diner, with the exception of the well-dressed man seated next to her who'd said he was a former colleague of the bride's. Her place on the aisle gave her a choice view of the arch that framed the glowing fireplace and the mantel decorated with white and red bows and holiday greenery. Better still, she had a prime view of the best man, decked out in an immaculate black tuxedo, his brown hair recently trimmed to perfection. Gavin O'Neal symbolized perfection in her eyes, even though the handsome groom was supposed to be the star of the show. But as far as she was concerned, Gavin was the most beautiful man in the room. Heck, the entire town. And for a little while he had been all hers.

As soft music began to filter through speakers set out about the room, the audience stood to welcome the bridal party. Valerie reluctantly turned her attention away from Gavin to the aisle, where she glimpsed the back of a tall, lithe woman dressed in a sleeveless green satin gown, her slender arms draped with a matching wrap, as she glided past the onlookers. Not long after, Melissa Mason appeared, her chestnut curls secured high on her head, her off-the-shoulder ecru lace wedding dress shimmering in the soft glow of the candles lining the walls. *Radiant* was the first thought that came to Valerie's mind as Melissa passed. *Totally in love* was the second when Melissa took Logan's hand in hers and gazed into his eyes.

Once they were seated again, Valerie's thoughts kept drifting away as the minister began the service. She allowed herself to imagine standing with Gavin, his hand in hers as he vowed to love and honor her all the days of their lives. Although her fantasies of ever after were simply that—fantasies—she refused to feel bad for having them since that was all she would ever have. She saw no real harm in indulging in the musings because no one else would ever have to know, especially not Gavin.

After the bride and groom engaged in the traditional kiss, the crowd broke out into applause and came to their feet again. Only then did Valerie get a good look at the maid of honor as she joined the best man to return down the aisle. The woman was gorgeous, with ample curves and a fall of dark hair that should be featured in a commercial. Gavin crooked his arm for the attendant to take, earning a smile from the lady, who now had a solid hold on the sheriff. Valerie's heart tumbled in her chest, and the beautiful red dress Gavin had chosen for her didn't seem beautiful at all. She despised her insecurity, hated that she felt as if she didn't belong at this event or with him. But when Gavin paused at her side on his way down the aisle and gave her hand a quick squeeze, for a fleeting moment Valerie did feel as if she really did belong with him. To him.

The pastor invited the audience to the dining area for the reception and they heeded the call en masse. Valerie worked her way through the crowd, searching for Gavin, who wasn't anywhere within her view. She briefly wondered if the dishonorable maid had carted him off to another room so they could get to know each other better.

On top of the bite of jealousy, Valerie also experienced the sting of loneliness that had been such a prominent part of her life over the past few years. She considered taking a seat somewhere out of the way, until she heard, "I knew it would look great on you."

The comment drew Valerie around to face Alison Lind-Hartman, who'd recently married Mark Hartman, another member of Gavin's secretive group. Her winter-white formfitting suit enhanced her flawless warm-chocolate skin and showcased her elegant carriage. Now Valerie truly felt short, insignificant and definitely scrappy. Yet she'd grown very fond of Alli in recent months, so she certainly couldn't fault her for anything, particularly since she seemed to be involved somehow in the selection of Valerie's new dress.

Intent on covering her stupid lack of confidence, Valerie propped both hands on her hips and smiled. "Let me guess. You got roped into going shopping with the sheriff."

Alli shrugged. "Mark asked me to help Gavin out. He seemed pretty desperate for some womanly advice."

"You did a great job." Valerie drew Alli into a brief hug and told her, "Thanks so much."

Alli returned her smile. "It wasn't a problem at all. I'm just glad I guessed your size correctly."

Valerie was glad to have Alli's company. "Where's that beautiful baby?"

Alli pointed behind her. "She's with Mark right now. We hadn't planned to bring her, but Mark's niece isn't feeling well. I think she might have the flu."

Didn't everyone? "I can relate to that."

"I know," Alli said. "Gavin told me you'd been very sick. In fact, you're all he talked about today. He's got it bad for you."

Valerie definitely had it bad for him. "He's been a wonderful friend." And the best of lovers.

"Mama! Mama!"

Valerie looked down to see fifteen-month-old Erika wrap her chubby arms around Alli's slender legs.

"There you are!" Alli swept Erika into her arms, popped a kiss on the toddler's cheek and balanced her on one hip. "What have you been up to, baby girl?"

Valerie reached over and took Erika's tiny hand. "Hey, honey. You're getting so big."

Erika grinned, flashing a deep dimple. "Cookie?"

Valerie laughed over Erika's usual request. "Sorry, sweetie, I left them at the diner. But when your mama brings you in, I'll be sure to have one waiting for you."

When Erika began to squirm and called for her daddy, Alli released her and she took off through the crowd, sprinting as fast as her little legs would allow.

"She's such a joy," Alli said. "I don't know what we'd do without her."

Valerie looked beyond Alli to see Mark holding Erika above his head, causing her to let go a raucous belly laugh. "She looks so much like your husband."

Alli glanced back, then smiled at Valerie. "Yes, she does. But Mark and his brother favored, too. That's why Erika could easily be mistaken for Mark's biological child."

"Are you and Mark still planning to adopt Erika?" Valerie asked.

"Definitely. We know that's what Mark's brother and his wife would have wanted. But we don't have a home study scheduled until February because of a shortage of available caseworkers. As much as I want it to happen, the whole process makes me nervous."

A process that was very familiar to Valerie. "I'm sure you'll do fine, Alli. Caseworkers love adoptions. That's the best part of the job."

Alli gave her a questioning look. "You sound like you've had some experience."

"I have," Valerie admitted. "I was studying social work before my grandmother passed away. I did some interning with Social Services. I hope to go back to it eventually and finish up."

As soon as she put together her own past in order to help others deal with theirs.

"You should go back," Alli said. "As much as I love taking care of Erika, I'm glad to be in school."

When someone called her name, Alli turned and nodded before bringing her attention back to Valerie. "I guess I should join my husband now. He looks like he could use some help with Erika."

Valerie waved a hand in dismissal. "Go ahead. I'll see if I can find Gavin. He's probably off somewhere talking with friends." She hoped that was who he was with and not the maid of honor.

"I think that's why Mark's calling me," Alli said. "He mentioned something about a few of the guys having a brief meeting to discuss whatever it is they usually discuss."

Valerie suspected it had something to do with the murder investigation, and she also suspected that Alli knew exactly what it was all about. Probably one of the perks of being a Cattleman's Club wife. "Then I'll go mingle for a while."

"I'll catch up with you in a while." Alli hugged Valerie again and set off to join Mark near the buffet table.

Valerie considered grabbing a bite to eat, maybe even a glass of champagne, but her stomach hadn't quite returned to normal. Or maybe the heaviness had to do with her sudden melancholy. Everyone in the house seemed to be paired up, and although she was technically with Gavin, she wasn't really *with* him, at least not for much longer.

As soon as she had the opportunity, and her car back on Monday, she intended to seriously seek what she'd been looking for, then return to St. Louis to get on with her life—without the sheriff—even knowing she would never be the same again.

Gavin had spent the past hour in a private room filled with fellow Cattleman's Club members, receiving surveillance reports on Gretchen Halifax that amounted to nothing, as well as being the brunt of several jokes about his relationship with Val. Now all he wanted to do was find his girl and get home.

He spotted her sitting in a fancy gold chair in the corner of the living room without any company, hands folded tightly in her lap. At that moment he hated himself for leaving her alone for so long without any explanation. But he'd wanted to get the meeting over with as soon as possible so he could get to the next phase of the evening—his second surprise.

As Gavin crossed the room, Val glanced up and met his gaze. She looked genuinely pleased to see him, and he was definitely happy to see her. He knelt before her and laid his hands on hers. "You still feeling okay?" he asked.

She rubbed her thumb along his wrist. "I'm fine. They're cutting the cake now and I hear they're going to be tossing the bouquet, which means the garter comes next. You might want to get in there and give it a go."

Gavin shook his head. "Can't say that I'm interested in any of that."

She rested a hand on her chest. "What? You don't want to watch the single women fighting over a bunch of flowers like desperate alley cats?"

"I don't think that's going to be much of a competition considering the lack of single women here tonight. Unless you're going to do it."

"No, not me." She looked away. "Melissa's maid of honor will probably be there. What's her name?"

"Madison."

"Oh, so you two are on a first-name basis?" Her smile looked forced. "You work fast, Sheriff."

Gavin couldn't believe she sounded so jealous and he had to admit he was kind of pleased by that. Male pride, plain and simple. "Look, Val, I talked to her for about two minutes. I also met her husband."

Now she looked chagrined. "I didn't realize she was married."

"She is. And even if she wasn't, I'm not interested." He stood and pulled her to her feet. "I'm only interested in one lady, and she's coming home with me right now."

When he started tugging her toward the entry, she pulled him to a stop. "Aren't you even going tell the bride and groom goodbye?"

Good point, but he'd call Logan in a couple of days, apologize and tell him Valerie was still under the weather. That might not be the case, but he did plan to get her under the covers real soon. "He'll understand."

After retrieving their coats from the hall closet, Gavin made sure Val was sufficiently wrapped up before he led her outside to the SUV. Even though Logan was his neighbor, several acres and a couple of miles separated their ranches, so walking wasn't an option. Even if it had been, he would've taken his vehicle to shorten the time it took to arrive at his house.

They drove in easy silence, Val's head tipped against his shoulder, her hand firmly in his. Since the weather had turned warmer, only a few drifts of snow remained on the side of the road. At least the conditions weren't conducive for more weather-related accidents. Tonight he wanted no interruptions whatsoever and he'd told his deputies that very thing. He only hoped they would adhere to his request.

After they pulled into the drive, Gavin cut off the engine and turned to Val. "After we get out, I want you to do everything I ask, no questions."

She frowned. "What's this all about?"

"I said no questions." He gave her a quick kiss. "Trust me, you'll know soon enough." Or at least he hoped she would. He'd relied on assistance to execute the second part of his plan, and if that hadn't panned out, someone was in big trouble. Specifically a group of teenage jocks.

Gavin rounded the hood and helped Val out of the truck, showed her to the front door, then took a red bandanna from his jacket pocket. "I'm going to put this on you for a few minutes."

She eyed the bandanna then surprisingly smiled. "Why, Sheriff, are you getting kinky on me?"

He rubbed his chin. "Actually not at the moment, but we could consider using the blindfold later. Not a bad idea at that. But first…" He stepped behind her, covered her eyes with the kerchief and tied it. "Is that okay?" he asked when he stepped back in front of her.

"If you mean can I see anything, no."

"Good." Gavin unlocked the front door and guided Val through the foyer and into the great room. Just as he'd planned, the surprise he'd designed solely for her benefit had been carried out down to the last detail—every multicolored ornament and flashing light strategically placed on the twelve-foot fir set near the window.

He shrugged out of his jacket and took off her coat, then tossed them on the sofa. Taking her hand, he led her to the tree and loosened the knot binding the bandanna. "Okay, I'm going to take this off now and you tell me what you think."

When he dropped the blindfold from her eyes, she sucked in a sharp breath. "Oh, my gosh, it's beautiful." Her tone sounded awed, almost reverent.

He stood beside her, her hand curled into his. "It could use a few more ornaments, but it was the best I could do in the time that I had."

She slipped her arm around his waist and leaned her head against his shoulder. "Is this what you really did when you disappeared tonight?"

"Nope. I hired a few elves. Actually some of the kids who have gotten into trouble lately. Just minor offenses, vandalism, that sort of thing, including the boy that was involved in the wreck the other day."

Val looked as shocked as she had been when she'd first viewed the tree. "You let them in your house when you weren't here?"

"Yeah. I figured I'd give them a chance to work off their debt to society by doing this. After they finished, they were supposed to go over to the convalescent home and help the Historical Society ladies hand out gifts to the residents."

She turned into his arms and kissed his cheek. "Just one question, Sheriff. Where have you been keeping your white horse?"

He grinned. "In the closet with my white hat."

"You are just full of surprises tonight."

"And I'm not done yet." Taking her hand in his, he led her to the hearth and flipped on the switch that illuminated the fireplace. "I thought you'd appreciate this one the most."

Gavin watched Val's gaze track upward to where the green construction-paper Christmas tree, decorated with misshapen glitter ornaments, hung above the mantel. He watched the wonder pass over her expression and her hand flutter to her mouth.

Moving behind her, he circled his arms securely around her waist. "This is compliments of Mrs. Brady's third-grade class. I spoke to them last month about the job, and she returned the favor by making this a special art project." He pointed at the tree. "I like the star at the top, even though they did leave the *E* off the end of your name. Kind of gives it a special charm, don't you think?"

Again Val faced him, her blue eyes clouded with tears. "I think this is probably the most wonderful thing anyone has ever done for me."

"It's only fair considering what you've done for me."

She lowered her gaze. "I haven't done anything for you, Gavin, except get sick and borrow your car and your guest room."

"You're so wrong, Val. You've brought a lot to my life." He pulled her against his chest, close to his hammering heart, and tipped her chin up. "It's been seventeen years since I've had holiday decorations in my house, and I thought it might bother me. But seeing the look on your face, knowing how much it means to you, it makes me feel great. At peace, I guess you could say, for the first time since my parents' deaths."

"I'm glad." She said it softly and with a sadness Gavin couldn't ignore.

He drew in a deep breath in preparation to tell her exactly what he was feeling. A first for him. "I love you, Val."

Taking him totally by surprise, she wrested out of his arms and turned her back to him. "There's something I have to tell you, Gavin."

Considering her serious tone, he had a gut-level feeling that he might not want to hear that *something*. Namely she didn't feel the same about him. "Val, look at me." When she slowly turned to him, he said, "Whatever it is you have to tell me, if it's not good news, it can wait until morning."

She studied the slate floors and kneaded her hands. "I don't think it should wait."

He definitely didn't want to get into this, at least not right now. "Do you have some kind of disease?"

Val's gaze zipped to his. "No, that's not it."

"A husband or boyfriend waiting for you somewhere?"

"No. Nothing like that."

He brought her back into his arms. "Then that's all I need to know. Right now, I want to make love to you, unless you don't want that."

Gavin held his breath until she said, "I want that more than anything. And you're right, it can wait until morning."

Now that Gavin had told her he loved her, Valerie knew it was wrong to put off the inevitable. But at the moment she didn't care about right or wrong. She only cared about being with him this final time. Still, when tomorrow arrived, she would answer his gifts with one of her own—the truth.

Right then, her focus centered on Gavin standing behind her in the great room, a glowing fire and the blinking lights providing the perfect backdrop, several blankets and pillows laid out on the floor providing the perfect place to make love. He slid the zipper down, parting the fabric and taking the dress with him as he glided his warm lips down her spine. After turning her around, he kissed his way back up her body, pausing to press his mouth against the sheer triangle of her panties. He stood and rimmed a finger beneath the lace band securing the stockings at her thighs. "All night I imagined you wearing these and nothing else," he said, his voice incredibly low, intoxicating. "I want you to leave them on."

"All right," Valerie said, all she could manage as he effortlessly removed her bra and tossed it aside.

Gavin seated her on the edge of the sofa and removed her heels before taking his place beside her. He worked his boots and socks off, then came to his feet to face her, shedding his tuxedo one article at a time at an agonizingly slow pace. When he finally stripped out of his briefs, Valerie's stomach was tangled in nervous knots of anticipation and a strong heat had settled between her thighs.

She was completely captivated by the feel of his callused hands skimming up her legs to her panties that he soon slid away. He nudged her back on the sofa and knelt before her.

"You're shaking," he said as he splayed his palm across her trembling belly.

She smoothed a fingertip over the cleft in his chin. "It's not because of any kind of illness, I promise. It's just being here like this, with you."

He captured her lips in a gentle kiss before finding her gaze once more. "I've wanted this all week." He twined his fingers with hers. "Us, together again."

So had Valerie. Little else had occupied her mind today. "So have I. In fact, I had all this energy last night and I started to wake you. But I knew you hadn't slept all that well when I was sick, so I didn't have the heart."

"I wasn't too tired to make love with you. I never will be." His expression turned somber. "I want to make you happy, Val. I want you to feel better than you've ever felt before. Not only tonight but every time I make love with you."

Little did he know, this would probably be the last time. "You already make me feel that way, Gavin."

"But I want to do more." He nuzzled his face between her breasts. "I plan to do more." He lifted his head and studied her eyes. "Do you trust me?"

"Yes." And she did, with her very life.

"Then just hold on to me."

He pulled her forward until her hips were at the edge of the cushions and parted her legs. With one hand clasped tightly with hers and the other beneath her bottom, he leaned forward and trailed his warm lips down her body. She knew exactly where he was going and what he was about to do. She also recognized that to trust him with this much familiarity was totally foreign to her. But she had all the faith in the world that he would take her to a plane she'd never been before, a place she wouldn't easily forget, as if she could ever forget anything he'd done for her to this point.

Valerie would never forget his incredible skill either, she thought when he made the first gentle pass of his tongue over her sensitive flesh. Never forget the heady feeling of being totally at his command, everything bared to him without reservation. He knew exactly where to center his attention, precisely how much pressure to apply to keep her balanced on the threshold of coming apart before he backed off ever-so-slightly. Just when she thought she might actually go insane with the need for completion, he did it again, teasing her into a mindless fervor, only this time he grew more insistent with his competent mouth.

When the demands of her body began to take over, Valerie gripped Gavin's hand tightly, her erratic heartbeat echoing in her ears. And with the glide of his finger inside her, the deep pull of his lips, the climax barreled down on her with such force her whole body jerked.

His name left her mouth in a harsh whisper, her breath following in a series of ragged pants. A steady stream of tremors continued long after her respiration returned to normal, and she wondered if she would ever recover.

Gavin released her hand and left her, bringing Valerie back around to the here and now. She opened her eyes to find him taking care with a condom before coming back to her. He lifted her legs and pulled her knees to his chest, then joined his body to hers with a deep thrust. He emitted so much power, so much strength, so much raw sexuality that Valerie could only watch him in awe. Watch his dark gaze connect with hers. Watch the glow of the flames play across his beautiful face.

Then suddenly he completely withdrew from her. "This isn't what I want."

An edge of panic threatened to destroy her blissful mood. "What's wrong?"

"I want to be closer to you," he said as he held out his hand. "I want you close to me."

Valerie experienced another bout of persistent tears, but she blinked them back as she'd learned to do so well. She could cry later, after he was asleep and unaware that she wept for what they could never have together. "I'm all for being closer."

Gavin whispered, "Come here," then guided her to the make-shift bed on the floor before the fire. He laid her back gently, then moved atop her. Without hesitating, he guided himself inside her again, this time wrapping her securely in his hold, kissing her softly, touching her with such gentleness that Valerie feared she might cry whether she cared to or not.

But Gavin soon turned her attention to him as he used his hands and his own body to bring her back into the realm of pure sensation. Valerie had often heard women talk behind their hands about being consumed by passion in the arms of a lover, and before now she'd always scoffed. Because of Gavin, she understood that completely, due to her absolute conversion into a truly carnal being.

He had no qualms about taking their lovemaking to a wilder level and letting it be known that his sole aim was to lift her right over the edge with him. Driven by her newfound sense of daring, her need to please him as he'd pleased her, Valerie mustered all her strength and rolled until she was seated on top of him.

Gavin tangled his hands in her hair as his look of surprise melted into a half smile. "Oh, yeah."

She responded with her own, "Oh, yeah," and a suggestive shift of her hips. He lifted toward her again and again, their bodies damp and slick from their efforts and their hands in constant motion over each other. After a time, Valerie picked up the pace, saw Gavin's eyes go nearly black, felt his frame growing rigid beneath her. With another hard upward thrust of his hips, she climaxed, and so did he.

Valerie collapsed against Gavin's chest, her arms limp at his sides and her cheek resting near his shoulder. He tightened his hold on her, one hand gently cradling her head, the other caressing her back. They stayed that way for a long while, content to hold each other, touch each other. She had never known such peace, had never experienced such contentment, and she didn't want it to end.

But end it must, that much she realized. Still, she had more than a few memories to carry home with her and maybe, just maybe, that would be enough. It would have to be enough. What other choice did she have?

Gavin lifted her head and kissed her with the sweet, sweet tenderness she'd come to know so well in his arms. "As much as I like the floor," he said, "I think we should go to bed now."

She allowed him to help her up, their arms wrapped around each other's waists as he guided her into his bedroom, then into his bed, where she took the spot she'd occupied for the past several nights.

When he went into the bathroom, Valerie rolled to her side, facing the window so he wouldn't see how much he had affected her. She clamped her hand over her mouth to muffle the sobs and tugged the covers up to her shoulders to drive away the cold, but neither worked. She willed herself to stop crying with the last of her declining control.

Gavin returned a brief time later and settled against her back, the way he had on those nights when she'd been racked with fever and out of her mind. Tonight she didn't have a fever—at least not the kind brought about by the flu. But she must be out of her mind for not blurting out the truth before he had changed her mind with his declaration.

First thing tomorrow she would tell him. In the morning, in the harsh light of day.

After a time the sound of Gavin's steady breathing, the loosening of his physical hold on her, told her that he'd fallen asleep. She memorized this moment and accepted that with the dawn came the end of her temporary paradise. And even though he wouldn't be able to hear her, she whispered what was first and foremost on her mind and in her heart. "I love you, too, Gavin."

In a not-quite-awake haze Gavin opened his eyes to find Valerie had rolled away from him onto her back, one arm raised above her head on the pillow, the other draped across her abdomen. The faint light filtering through the window washed her features in a muted glow, a face that he wanted to see every morning and every night from this point forward. While she slept, he continued to watch her, immersed in the absolute need to protect her from anything and everything. He loved her more than he could say, wanted her more than anything he'd ever wanted in his lifetime. Quietly he inched closer and buried his face in her hair, driven by the need to touch her. If he had his way, they'd stay in bed all day long, with no interruptions. They could have their little talk, and if luck prevailed, she would tell him she loved him, too. Provided she did love him. His instincts kept telling him that was true. But then, his instincts hadn't always come through for him, particularly when it came to matters of the heart.

The shrill ring of the phone thrust Gavin into reality and away from her. Yet he still kept one hand on her arm as he rolled over and snatched up the receiver from the nightstand. For some illogical reason he worried that if he let her out of his sight even for a few moments, he might never see her again.

He barked out an irritable, "What?" on the heels of his frustration.

"Sorry to bother you, Sheriff, but this is Bill Rhodes down at the garage. I have something you need to take a look at. It has to do with the waitress's car. I found it when I put it up on the rack."

Gavin shot a look at Val, who was inspecting his overhead fan, her eyes still clouded with sleep. "Is it bad?"

"Oh, yeah, you could say that. That's why you need to get down here ASAP."

So much for staying in bed all day. "It can't wait until tomorrow?"

"No, it can't. And I don't think it's a good idea to discuss it on the phone."

None of this made much sense, but Bill Rhodes wasn't the type to make that kind of a request unless it was serious. "Give me ten minutes." He hung up the phone, deciding that it would be best to check out the problem first, before he let Val in on it.

Considering the way she looked right now—totally content for the first time since he'd known her—he decided it could wait.

"I've got to go," he said as he pushed off the bed. "Some business I need to take care of."

She sat up, hugging the covers to her like a security blanket. "What about our talk, Gavin?"

He pulled a set of clean clothes from the closet. "We'll talk when I get back."

"I promised Manny I'd work the Sunday lunch shift."

He set his clothes aside on the bureau, rounded the bed and kissed her softly. "I shouldn't be gone that long," he said before heading into the bathroom for a quick shower.

At least he hoped it wouldn't take long. When he returned, Gavin planned to listen to Val's confessions, let her get it off her chest—whatever *it* was—and make love to her again. And again. He would make it perfectly clear that he loved her and he wanted to be with her permanently. Nothing she could do or say would ever change that. Nothing.

Ten

As she sat in the kitchen and watched the time grow closer to her shift at the diner, Valerie decided that Gavin probably wouldn't make it back for their heart-to-heart before she had to go into work. Fate, for some unknown reason, was preventing her from finally baring her soul. But then, fate probably knew that when she did finally come clean, that could be the end of her time with the sheriff.

She tapped her foot beneath the dinette table for a few minutes before deciding she needed to prepare for the inevitable departure. Scooting the chair back, she trudged down the hall and, once inside the bedroom, pulled the boxes from the closet and her bag from beneath the bed. She opened the top drawer, removed her keepsake chest and withdrew the faded letter that she'd discovered in the small wooden chest, along with the pendant, following her grandmother's death.

If you have possession of this letter, that means I have long since passed from this earth and you are my descendant. I rely on you now to seek the truth, and please know that what I have done in my past, I did so because I had no choice.

Many years ago I resided in Royal, Texas, yet I was charged with crimes I did not commit. You will discover my story in a diary, along with a map indicating the place where I hid the stolen gold, located in my father's house beneath a floorboard in the small closet in the parlor. You will also find with the gold the answers to what happened the night I confronted my father's killer, the town's revered mayor. You must place my pendant over the exact heart on the map, then look for the willow tree bearing the initials J.G. and B.W. There you will find the treasure, buried at the base of the tree, right beneath the symbol of our love.
Godspeed,
Jessica Baker/Jessamine Golden

Valerie pocketed both letters to show them to Gavin later and put the heart pendant around her neck. Oddly none of it seemed to matter anymore. Not in light of Gavin's declaration last night that kept playing over and over in her mind like a favorite song.
I love you, Valerie…
But would his love be enough to take them past her deception? Would he understand why she had done what she'd done? Why she had kept the truth from him? She had no choice but to find out as soon as they were together again.

On that thought, she took out her own journal to write what could be the final chapter of her life with Gavin.

Well, I've been through a lot since my last writing. Gavin took care of me when I had the flu, took me to a wedding, bought me my very own Christmas tree and told me he loved me. I want to hope that his love will be strong enough to lead him to acceptance. I want to believe that I can have a future with this man who is so strong and honorable and easy to love. But after I tell him everything, he might not want me. Still, I will continue to hope until all hope is gone.

* * *

In the back room of the headquarters of the Texas Cattleman's Club, Gavin was surrounded by four men who pretended to concentrate on the business at hand. But he could see the pity in their eyes and he could almost read their minds. *Poor guy. He's been suckered by a woman.* They would be right.

Regardless, decisions had to be made over what to do next. For that reason he slid the plastic bag containing the gun into the middle of the conference room table. "Bill Rhodes found this taped to the wheel well in Valerie's car. It's a thirty-eight. The serial number's been filed off, but it's a match to the gun that killed Durmorr."

Tom leaned forward, his hands clasped tightly together. "Then you're thinking Valerie killed him?"

Gavin wasn't sure what to think. But Valerie Raines in the role of murderer was unthinkable. "She could have been set up. Someone could have planted the gun."

The whole lot of them looked skeptical, but Gavin wasn't willing to give up on her just yet. There had to be a logical explanation.

"What else do we know about her?" Mark asked.

"I had Vincente expedite a background check through the police department computers while I was at Rhodes's garage with the forensics team, just to see if anything turned up." A report which Gavin deliberately hadn't seen yet. "Did you get it, Jake?"

"I picked it up on my way here." Jake's uneasy demeanor as he withdrew the report from his pocket led Gavin to believe he might not want to know the content.

"Last known residence is St. Louis," Jake began. "She was raised by her grandmother from the age of seven after being abandoned by her mother. The grandmother passed away last year. She graduated from college and she's been working on a master's degree in social work while serving as a counselor at a youth center."

At least she'd been truthful about her grandmother, Gavin thought, even though he didn't understand why she hadn't told him more details about her education. Of course, that would have blown her waitress cover. "What else?"

"Her mother is Carla Raines and she's currently incarcerated in a prison in Indiana serving a life sentence," Jake continued.

Gavin swallowed hard. "On what charge?"

"Murder charges," Jake said, confirming Gavin's suspicions. "Seems she was involved in a convenience-store robbery. The clerk was shot and killed, although they don't think she pulled the trigger. But she was definitely there."

Dammit! Why hadn't Val told him that? Easy. He might have assumed that old adage that the apple doesn't fall far from the tree—or at least she would have thought that. With good reason, considering their conversations about his intolerance to crime. She still didn't have the right to deceive him. And with any luck, that was the end of the secrets, at least when it came to her history. "Is that it?"

Jake tugged at his tie. "No, and you're not going to like it."

Gavin braced for the worst possible scenario. "Spill it."

"She has a juvenile record. It's sealed, so we don't know what kind of crime she committed."

Even though this was looking real bad for Val, Gavin still couldn't imagine her hurting anyone. But then, he obviously didn't know her at all or what she might be capable of. For several nights she'd been in his bed, in his home, all the while lying to him. Pretending to care about him. What else had she lied about?

Tom cleared his throat, a sure sign of his discomfort. "Do you have any reason to believe she had a connection with Durmorr?"

Oh, yeah, Gavin did. "She said she had a couple of run-ins with him. They also lived at the motor court at the same time."

"Then maybe this was some sort of revenge thing," Connor offered. "Maybe he got rough and she decided to defend herself."

"If that had been the case, then why didn't she come forward?" Tom asked. "When we found Durmorr's body, we didn't see any sign of anyone else around."

Now Gavin had to reveal another piece of incriminating evidence he'd discovered when he'd returned to the house to confront her only to find she'd already left for work. "I came upon this in a box." He fished through his jacket, pulled out the black cap etched with the initials S.L.Y.C. and tossed it next to the gun.

They all leaned over to take a look before Tom said, "That's the cap from the surveillance tape at the museum. The woman who stole the map was wearing it."

"Borrowed the map," Gavin said, earning a few more looks from his colleagues. "She did return it." Now he sounded like a lovesick idiot defending his lady to the end, despite what she might have done.

"She probably made a copy," Jake said.

"She did," Gavin admitted. "I found it in her room. And that leads me to believe she's looking for the gold." Motivated by greed, he'd guess, like most criminals. But was it greed or had she just grown tired of being without? It didn't matter. She'd still lied to him about it.

"We all know that Durmorr probably murdered Devlin because of that gold," Connor added. "Which means Valerie could be involved in that, as well."

Gavin didn't even want to think about that possibility. "Or it could be she connected with Durmorr after that." *Still hanging on to hope, Sheriff,* their expressions seemed to say. And in a way Gavin was. He wanted this nightmare to end with the knowledge that Valerie had been set up to take a fall for the real killer, even if she had been searching for buried treasure. But he still held more evidence that could nail her to the wall.

Gavin lifted the cap for inspection. "There are a few stray hairs caught in the back clasp. I'll have them compared to the ones found on Devlin's body, at least microscopically for the time being. We'll have to get a court order to run the DNA, which shouldn't be a problem."

"And if they prove to be hers?" Mark asked.

"Then it looks like we have our killer." And Gavin would have to arrest the woman he had fallen in love with. As stupid as it seemed, he still loved her—or at least loved the woman he'd thought her to be. He couldn't make himself believe the worst until he was absolutely forced to do that.

"Where is she now?" Jake asked.

Gavin checked his watch. "She's at the diner, but she should be at the house in a couple of hours. And when she gets back, I'll be waiting for her."

Valerie walked into the great room to find Gavin seated in the chair, one leg crossed over the other at the ankles. By all appearances he looked relaxed, until she noticed his grave expression. Something had gone terribly wrong, and she intended to find out the details.

After tossing her purse aside, she collapsed onto the sofa and stretched her sore legs out in front of her. "Tough day, I take it."

"You could say that."

She heard no warmth in his tone. In fact, he sounded as cold as the ice that had recently melted from the rooftops. "Come on, Gavin. It will help if you talk to me about it."

"I intend to." He remained as still as stone as he said, "I know all about your mother."

Valerie's whole being went on red alert. "I was going to tell you about her last night, but you stopped me, remember?"

"You should have told me a long time ago," he said. "I had a right to know."

The familiar shame tried to take over, but this time she refused to let it. "Actually it was my decision if and when to tell you. I wanted you to know after—" *I fell in love with you* "—we'd become close. I've learned it's not something you readily share with people, especially people who might not understand."

He released a cynical laugh. "Guess you're going to tell me I didn't have a right to know about your criminal record either, even though I opened my house to you."

Now she was angry. "Mind telling me why you suddenly decided to investigate my background?"

"First, another question. Do you own a gun?"

That caused her to straighten in her seat. "No. I hate guns. Why?"

He put his boots flat on the floor, then leaned forward, forearms draped on his knees, hands fisted together. "Then would you mind telling me why Rhodes found one taped underneath your car? Specifically the gun that murdered Malcolm Durmorr."

She simply stared at him a few moments until the shock settled some. "I have no idea why it's there, but I assure you I didn't put it there."

"But you did know Durmorr." He didn't bother to disguise the suspicion in his tone.

"I barely knew him," she said. "And if you think I killed him because he came on to me, you have totally lost your mind."

"Maybe so, but you should be able to understand why I might have my doubts."

"I see. We're back to once a criminal, always a criminal. Would you like to know what I did in my youth, Sheriff?"

He sat back and assumed an almost insolent posture. "Yeah. Enlighten me."

After coming to her feet, Valerie crossed the small space and stared down on him. "First of all, let me ask you a question. Have you ever had to listen to kids on the playground call your mother a jailbird?"

"No."

"Of course not. You had perfect parents who loved you and cared for you. Which leads to another question. Have you ever done without any necessities? Food? Clothes? Heat?"

His gaze faltered. "Not that I recall."

Tears burned hot behind her eyes, but she willed them away. "Then you don't know what it's like to be hungry or cold or not have enough money to buy the simple things. But I know that all too well."

"I'm really sorry about that, Val," he said without even a hint of true understanding. "But being poor doesn't give you a right to commit a crime."

"Spoken like a man who's never wanted for anything," she said through gritted teeth. "And for your information, I was fifteen years old when I was charged with shoplifting a coat. Not for me, for my grandmother. She was recovering from pneumonia and it was so cold, outside and inside our ratty apartment. *She* was cold. I went into a department store, grabbed a coat off the rack and tried to wear it out."

The memories came back then, pelting her like a hailstorm, as hard and unforgiving as Gavin's expression. "I'd never shopped anywhere but in thrift stores, so I didn't know about sensors. I got caught. They cuffed me and put me in a patrol car. I got charged with a crime and my grandmother still didn't have a decent coat. Pretty ironic, huh?"

Gavin rubbed his forehead but didn't say a word.

"So there you have it, Sheriff," she continued. "I was a teenage thief, but I've done nothing—*nothing*—but walk the straight and narrow since then. A lot of good that's done me."

Gavin sat in silence for a few moments, his gaze focused on the window, before he finally looked at her again. "Are you sure you haven't committed any more crimes?"

Damn his indifference. "I definitely did not kill Malcolm Durmorr, whether you choose to believe that or not."

He withdrew her youth-center baseball cap from his pocket and dangled it from one finger. "You were caught on a surveillance camera stealing a map from a museum display, wearing this. The map that's supposed to lead to buried treasure. I figure you thought you'd done without long enough and you decided to pad your pockets with some gold. When Durmorr got in your way, you took care of that."

This time Valerie looked away. "If you recall, I left a note of apology for *borrowing* the map after I returned it. And as far as your assumptions about me being some kind of greedy fortune hunter, that's not at all true."

He stuffed the cap back into his pocket and leveled a hard gaze on her. "What is the truth, Valerie? Or do you even know the difference between truth and lies?"

Valerie. Now they were back to being virtual strangers. "The truth is, I'm Jessamine Golden's great-great-granddaughter. I came here in search of answers, not the damn gold. Those answers are supposed to be buried with the treasure, and that's all I care about. I didn't plan to move into your house and I certainly didn't plan to fall in love with you."

Gavin seemed more surprised by that revelation than any of the others. "Why the hell didn't you tell me all of this sooner?"

If only she had, then maybe it wouldn't have come to this. "I tried, several times as a matter of fact, beginning with that first night in front of the fire. First you gave me your opinions about criminals. Then you told me you didn't want to know about my past. That my slate was wiped clean. Or have you forgotten about that?"

"You should have forced the issue."

"Probably so, but the last time I confided in a man I cared about, I regretted it. I suited him just fine as a lover, but when he went home on the weekends, he wouldn't take me. He said his mother would ask too many questions, and he couldn't tell her about my past. Which basically meant I wasn't good enough for him, except in bed, and that made me his whore."

Her tears began to flow then, tears of frustration and fear and anger. Of a deep-seated hurt the likes of which he'd never known. "So you see, I had to know if what they say about Jess is true, hoping and praying it's wrong, because then maybe I can believe that my mother's crimes are a fluke and that I won't be passing on some kind of tainted genes to my own children. I had to find out for myself before I can move forward with my life."

He met her gaze and she saw a flicker of compassion before it faded once more. "I would have understood."

She braced her palms on the chair's arms and leaned forward, her gaze locked into his. "Would you really have understood, Gavin? The man with zero tolerance to crime? Think about it. You probably would have locked me up as soon as you realized I was the one who took the map. Arrest first, ask questions later." She straightened and backed way from him, holding her arms tightly to her middle against the sudden chill. "Isn't that your policy, Sheriff?"

When he came to his feet slowly, grabbed his hat from the coffee table and brushed past her, she asked, "Where are you going?"

He stopped and turned, sporting the same emotionless expression. "I'm going to check out some more evidence, a few strands of hair we found on Durmorr's body. Blond hair."

Dear God, could this get any worse? But then again, they shouldn't match hers because she had been nowhere near Durmorr the night of his death. Unfortunately she had no one to vouch for her since she'd been in the motel alone.

"What then, Gavin?"

"If the strands match yours, then I'll be back to arrest you."

He might as well have knifed her right through the heart. "You do what you have to do, Gavin, and so will I."

He turned away from her. "In the meantime, I'll be gone at least an hour. Maybe longer."

Digging through her bag, she withdrew the keys to his car and dangled them from one finger. "Don't you want these?" she called out, prompting him to face her again. "You certainly wouldn't want to leave your car with a murderer and a thief, would you?"

"You keep them for now." He settled his hat on his head, completing his return to Old West avenger of justice, viewing her as the villain. "If you're innocent, you'll be here when I get back. If not, then take care of yourself."

As Gavin walked out the door, Valerie realized he was giving her a head start if she decided to run away. But she refused to run. She never had before.

She did intend to go on with her quest, beginning with locating the diary. If she found that and only that, she'd have another part of her great-great-grandmother's story. And the way things were shaping up, she might have to resort to reading it in prison unless she could somehow prove she had nothing to do with Malcolm Durmorr's murder.

Of course, she still had to retrieve the diary from the old Golden homestead, the one that had recently belonged to Jonathan Devlin.

Valerie shivered just thinking about going inside the house to search for the journal. And what if she couldn't locate the loose floorboard that supposedly served as its hiding place? What if someone had already found it? After all, the map had surfaced months ago. But if someone had found the diary, then where was it? All she could do was see if maybe it was still there, somehow overlooked.

If she did manage to get into the house, that would constitute breaking and entering. But what did she have to lose? Gavin believed she'd committed murder. He believed she was a career criminal, just like her mother. At one time he'd even believed that he loved her, but that no longer remained true, exactly as she'd predicted.

If the diary remained lost forever, she would try her best to locate the missing gold and turn it over to Gavin. And then she would fight for her life, battle for her freedom and prove to the world that she wasn't like her mother or Jessamine Golden. Even if she could never convince the man she would always love.

Her time was limited and it would soon be dark, so she had to hurry. She returned to her bedroom, laid out the letters for Gavin to see and wrote a last entry in her journal so he would know where to find her—and arrest her.

Valerie changed into jeans and a sweatshirt, grabbed a flashlight from the kitchen and borrowed Gavin's extra down coat. She immediately noticed it smelled like him, clean and fresh, providing her with some comfort as well as some sorrow.

Hurrying to the car, she fumbled twice with the keys before she finally got it started and headed away. Luckily she had a good sense of direction and had little trouble finding the location. When she arrived at the house, she pulled up the drive and parked out back, then rushed out of the car. The daylight had already faded, but she could make out enough to find the broken window and prayed that it hadn't been fixed yet. To her surprise, it lifted with ease and she climbed inside. Afraid of risking detection, she opted not to try the lights and instead flipped on the flashlight to discover she was in a bedroom where the furniture had been draped, giving the area a ghostly quality. She didn't believe in restless spirits, but then, she hadn't believed in true love until she'd met Gavin.

Shaking off all thoughts of the sheriff, determination kicked in, sending her into the hallway and eventually into the parlor. She shined the beam on the walls, searching for the closet door. Just when she thought she'd found it, "Are you looking for this?" came from behind her.

Valerie spun around and almost dropped the flashlight when she contacted the cool, gray eyes that now held a devilish gleam. She stepped back a few inches, widening the ray until she had the complete picture in view.

There Gretchen Halifax stood, immaculately dressed in a black fur coat, matching fur hat and black silk pants, a weathered journal in one hand, and a gun in the other—pointed straight at Valerie's head.

"Face it, O'Neal, you're still in love with her."

Gavin took his eyes from the road long enough to give Thorne a hard look. He appreciated Connor volunteering to come with him to arrest Valerie even if he didn't appreciate his assumptions. Correct assumptions. "It doesn't matter how I feel about her now. The hairs found on Devlin matched hers, and that means she's probably guilty of murder."

"But you're still not completely convinced," Connor said.

Gavin tightened his grasp on the steering wheel. "No."

"You're letting your emotions screw with your common sense, Gavin."

No use in arguing with Connor about that. Or arguing at all. His friends believed she was guilty and they could be right. But still…

"She never lied to me, exactly," Gavin said. "I never asked her if she had a record and I never pressed her for information about her past. And now that I think of it, she tried to tell me several times. I wouldn't let her."

"She withheld the truth by omission," Connor said. "But I can understand why you're trying to make excuses for her. If it were me and we were talking about Nita, I'd probably do the same thing."

Gavin shot a hard look at his friend before turning his attention to the road. Connor was a former army ranger, a hard-ass in most instances, but that was before he'd met his wife. Love did crazy things to men. Gavin had found that out the hard way.

Now only a mile from his ranch, he would know soon enough if Valerie was still there. As he turned up the drive, an overwhelming sense of dread filled him. He wasn't sure whether he wanted her to be there or if he hoped she'd taken off. Of course, she would eventually be found, but at least someone else could arrest her then.

Even though the sun had set, Gavin could still see that his dad's car was missing. Obviously she had left, and probably for good. But she wouldn't get far before the authorities would catch her—as soon as he made the call.

He wasn't quite ready to do that just yet, not until he confirmed her departure. Shifting the truck into Park, he kept it running and told Connor, "I'll be back in a minute." Without waiting for a response, Gavin sprinted to the front door, turned the key in the lock and rushed inside. He flipped on the lights as he went, as if he expected to find Val hiding in a corner, waiting for the big, bad sheriff to take her away.

When he found no sign of her in the kitchen, the great room or the loft, he immediately headed into the bedroom, expecting to find all of her things gone. Instead her bag rested on the end of the bed, only partially packed, and her uniforms still hung in the closet. She'd probably decided she wouldn't be needing those where she was going.

The wooden chest sitting on the top of the dresser immediately caught his attention. He couldn't imagine her leaving without that, but then, she had been in a hurry. Curious to see what it contained, he strode to the bureau to find two documents laid out on the oak surface beside it.

Gavin read the letter from Val's grandmother first, set that aside and picked up the yellowed parchment signed by Jessica

Baker—also known as Jessamine Golden. He scanned the letter
to learn the details about the gold, including the mention of a pendant. He remembered seeing Val wearing that pendant a few
months back, but not since she'd been in his house. That seemed
to be the key to the gold's exact location, along with the map,
which would explain why she had made the copy. He searched
the chest and found no sign of the necklace, which led him to
believe she had decided to search for the gold before she left
town. But if that were true, then why was the damn map still sitting on the corner of the bureau?

Gavin turned it around and immediately noticed that a black
X marked one of the hearts—the same hearts they'd puzzled over
for months. The gold's location. And next to the map he found
a small black journal opened up to a page containing neat script.

Gavin, if you're reading this now, I've gone to find the answers to my past. I promise you I had nothing to do with
Malcolm Durmorr's murder. I know you don't believe me,
but if you believe nothing else, please know that I love you
with all of my heart. That will remain true forever.

He collapsed onto the edge of the bed, holding the journal in
his hands, clinging to the final connection with Val. Right now
he didn't have time for this. He had to do his job, even if he suf-
fered from a heartache bigger than all of Royalton County. Bigger than Texas.

He had to suck it up and find her and he now knew where to
look. First, he'd go to the Devlin house, and if she wasn't there,
he'd move on to the Windcroft property. Even if she had decided
to flee after she found the gold, she would have to dig through
frozen ground, and that could take a lot of time.

Before he could heave himself off the bed, Connor appeared
in the doorway. "I take it she's not here."

Gavin shook his head. "No. But I know where she is and what
she's after." He nodded toward the bureau. "It's all spelled out
in that letter from Jess Golden, Val's great-great-grandmother."

Connor's gaze snapped from the documents to Gavin. "Then she's after the gold?"

"And a diary Jess left behind. It's been hidden in the Devlin house all these years."

Connor frowned. "That's got to be the diary Lucas Devlin mentioned to Tom. He found a reference to it in those notes when he was looking at Jonathan's books."

With all the mounting evidence, Gavin had forgotten about it. "I remember Lucas saying something about the feud being mentioned in the diary, but the letter talks about the mayor murdering Jess's father, and that's Edgar Halifax."

"Which paints a completely different picture of what everyone's believed about Halifax," Connor said. "If anyone in the family found out, then—"

"They'd be humiliated." Now it was all becoming too clear. "And even though that might not matter to some people, it would to Gretchen. She's all about appearances. My theory is Jonathan knew about it all along and for some reason threatened to release the information. Right in the middle of the mayoral campaign."

"That could be enough motivation for her to kill Jonathan," Connor said.

"She recruited Malcolm to help her because he was an outcast in the eyes of the Devlins. And she might have framed Val to cover up her own crimes," Gavin added. "Especially Durmorr's murder."

"Or Val and Gretchen could be working together," Connor said.

Gavin refused to believe that Val would involve herself in a murder scheme with the likes of Gretchen Halifax, even if he had witnessed a tense conversation between them the week before last. Whether that was his head talking or his heart, it didn't matter. He'd continue to believe in Valerie's innocence until proven otherwise. First, he needed to find her.

The dispatcher's voice calling Gavin from his portable radio jarred him back into action. Unhooking it from his belt, he depressed the button and said, "Go ahead."

"The deputies answered a ten-seventy in the county, Sheriff.

Rivera said you'd definitely want to know about it because it looks like arson."

Damn. Just what he needed on top of everything else, a suspicious fire. "What's the ten-twenty?"

"Jonathan Devlin's house."

Eleven

Many times during his law-enforcement career Gavin had witnessed destruction and degradation, a complete disrespect for human life through acts that defied both logic and decency. But not once during his career had he ever felt so sick—until now.

Just thinking that Valerie might somehow still be in the blazing inferno sent him into action, ignoring the nausea resting like a rock in his gut. He bolted from the SUV and into the ash raining all around, heading toward what was left of the house, until a hand gripped his shoulder and pulled him back.

"Don't do it, Gavin."

He turned and shook off Jake's grasp. He wasn't surprised to find him there. Putting out fires had always been Jake's calling, in every way possible. But tonight, Gavin damn sure wasn't going to let him interfere. Not if a chance remained that Val was still in the house. "I'm not going to let her die, Jake, I don't care—"

"She's not in there," Jake said. "Someone saw her leave about twenty minutes ago."

Gavin's mind whirled from confusion even while his frame relaxed from relief. "Then you're saying she set the place on fire?"

"I'm saying you need to talk to the witness."

Gavin followed Jake's gesture to a thin, elderly woman standing near two of his deputies, clutching a small terrier. Mrs. Velma Bradford, the neighbor who'd contacted them about the prowler.

He regarded Jake again, not quite ready to believe but more than ready to run into the burning building. "My car's on the street and I know she was driving it."

"We pushed it out of the drive so it wouldn't suffer any damage."

"But if Val's not in my car, then who did she leave with?"

Jake rested a hand on his shoulder. "Come talk to Mrs. Bradford. You're going to want to hear what she has to say."

Gavin wiped his eyes with the back of his arms, but his vision didn't want to clear. Just the soot and ash, the heat of the fire, nothing more. He didn't get emotional at scenes like this. He couldn't, for the sake of his own sanity. He had to stay grounded. He had to find Val.

When he reached the widow, Gavin held out his hand for her to take. "Good seeing you again, Mrs. Bradford. Mayor Thorne says you witnessed something tonight."

She set the dog on its feet and pulled her shawl close to her body. "Oh, yes, Sheriff. I was out walking my Winston and right before I went back in the house, I saw a woman drive up. That Gretchen woman who ran for mayor and thankfully didn't win." She shot Jake a toothy grin.

"Are you certain it was her?" Gavin asked.

"Yes. She drives that big white car. I think she's the one I've seen at the house before. Oddly she parked down the road a bit and then walked around back."

He tried to remain calm even though he wanted to get out of there and go find Val immediately. "Did you see anything after that?"

She scooped the whining, ancient dog into her arms. "I went into the house and looked out the windows. I saw another younger blonde drive up—" she pointed to Gavin's GTO "—in that car. She pulled in the drive all the way to the rear of the house. They were in there for about fifteen minutes before they left together in the white car."

Gavin's concern increased. "The younger blonde, did she look like she was leaving with the older woman willingly?"

Mrs. Bradford straightened to her full height. "No, she did not. In fact, it looked as if the other woman was practically dragging her to the car. She showed her to the driver's door and shoved her inside, then took off. That's when I saw the smoke and called 911."

Gavin patted Mrs. Bradford's back. "Thank you. You've been a big help."

"Will I have to make a statement?" she asked hopefully.

Thank God for nosy neighbors. "Definitely." Gavin gestured at Annie standing nearby. "Deputy Rivera will escort you into your house and write everything down."

"What now, O'Neal?"

When Gavin turned to find Connor standing behind him, he motioned him away from the milling crowd. "We need to get out of here immediately."

"Where are we going?"

"Back to your place. I know exactly where the gold is buried, thanks to Val."

"Then you're convinced it's on Windcroft land?"

"Yeah, and I'll tell you all the details on the way." First, Gavin had something important he had to attend to immediately. "Do you have your gun?"

Connor patted his coat. "Right here."

"Good. Now raise your right hand."

"What?"

"I don't have time for questions, dammit! Just do it."

When Connor slowly lifted his hand, Gavin said, "Do you swear to uphold the laws of Royalton County?"

"Well, yeah."

"Okay, you're deputized. Now let's get the hell out of here."

Connor hooked a thumb over his shoulder. "Why are you making me a deputy when you have all these men standing around?"

"I'll tell you in a minute." Gavin waited until he was behind the wheel and Connor was settled into the passenger seat before he explained. "If Val is somehow involved in this scheme with Gretchen, then I want you to arrest her because I can't do it. And if it came down to having to…" He couldn't even think it, much less say it. "I trust you to treat her with care."

But if Mrs. Bradford's poor eyesight hadn't deceived her, that meant Val could be Gretchen Halifax's next victim. And if Gretchen laid one hand on his lady, he'd shoot the murderous bitch first and ask questions later.

Many times during her experience with social work, Valerie had seen lost souls caught in the grip of confusion. But this was the first time she'd stared criminal madness—and evil—right in the eye. She was also staring down the barrel of a gun.

Gretchen kept the weapon trained on Valerie as she guided her through the winter-dry field, a shovel gripped in her fur-glove-covered hand. Valerie held the lone flashlight as they walked the perimeter of the small lake searching for the elusive willow etched with initials that had been carved there over a hundred years before. But was it still there? Maybe it had withered away with time. Maybe someone had even cut it down. But she didn't dare suggest that to her captor for fear that Gretchen would put the gun to good use.

The night air bit at Valerie's face where Gretchen had slapped her hard after she'd at first refused to tell her anything. Her only recourse had been to lead Gretchen to the hiding place and pray that she found an opportunity to escape. If not, she hoped that after Gretchen had her gold, she would let her go. Yet that seemed highly unlikely. The woman had killed before. She wouldn't hesitate to kill again—especially a witness.

"Shine the light on that tree," Gretchen said, her voice edgier than before.

Valerie complied, only to find a gnarled trunk and no initials. "That's not it."

Gretchen waved the gun. "Look on the other side. It's the only willow we've seen so far."

Rounding the tree, Valerie centered the beam on a massive knothole, and above that the letters B.W. and J.G., divided by a heart, carved into the ancient wood.

"This is it!" Now Gretchen's tone held a note of hysteria. "We've found it!"

Yes, they had found it, the place where Valerie's great-great-grandmother had been courted by the sheriff. How surreal that her own life had paralleled Jess's, right down to the impending arrest by the man that she loved. But where Jess had reportedly killed her lover, Valerie wouldn't dare harm a hair on Gavin's beautiful head. She'd rather die first. And she just might face that situation if she didn't find a way out of this whole mess.

"Grab some wood and build a fire," Gretchen demanded. "I can stay warm while you dig."

Valerie whipped around and shone the light on her. "I don't have any matches."

After leaning the shovel against the tree, Gretchen threw back her head and cackled like some horror-show creature. "How soon we forget that I've already started one fire tonight." She withdrew a slender gold lighter from her pocket.

Not only was the woman a murderer but she was also a pyromaniac. After Valerie handed over the flashlight, Gretchen aimed the beam on the ground while Valerie searched for kindling. As soon as she had a few sticks and limbs crisscrossed in a pile, then covered with leaves—something she'd learned during her stint as a counselor at a camp for troubled kids—she straightened and wiped her palms on her jeans. "It's all yours."

"Now take this lighter to start the fire. And don't do anything stupid."

After Valerie knelt before the wood, it took three attempts to spark the lighter—the same lighter Gretchen had used to set fire to the drop cloths covering the furniture at Jonathan Devlin's home. The flame flickered, then caught quickly, as if they'd been blessed by all the demons of hell. Not surprising considering the presence of the queen demon.

"Okay, it's done," Valerie said as she straightened. "What now?"

Gretchen dropped down onto a nearby fallen limb, laid the flashlight in her lap and withdrew Jess's diary, the gun still pointed at Valerie. She opened a page and chuckled. "Isn't this cute? All about how her father gave her a pony on her fifth birthday. Such useless drivel, don't you think?" Slowly, systematically, she tore the page from the diary, balled it up and tossed it into the fire.

Damn her! "I gather you don't like horses."

"I don't like sentimentality." She snapped the diary closed, stood again and then waved the flashlight at the shovel. "Start digging."

Valerie grabbed the tool and impaled the frozen ground, using all her weight, her fury and her feet to drive it deeper. Still, at this rate the excavation could take hours. Then again, that might not be a bad thing. If Gavin had returned to the house and found the map, he would know where to find her, and the fire would serve as a beacon. Or he could have assumed she'd fled, avoided her bedroom and issued an immediate APB on his former lover turned fugitive. A murdering, gold-digging femme fatale—or so he believed.

"How did you know I had the final clue to the gold?" she asked as she shoveled more dirt, resisting the urge to toss some on Gretchen's faux-fur hat.

"After I saw the pendant, which is outlined in the diary, I put it all together," she said. "In fact, I did a little research and I know all about you. How does it feel to be the great-great-granddaughter of an outlaw and the daughter of a murderer?"

How does it feel to be a murderer? Valerie wanted to say but refrained. "I haven't seen my mother in years. She doesn't matter anymore." Oh, but she did. She always had, despite her flaws. Still, Valerie couldn't change the past.

Gretchen moved closer to the fire, casting her black fur coat in an eerie blue glow. She looked like a feral cat, ready to pounce. "You know, Valerie, considering your criminal record, there's obviously a little of her in you. Maybe even a lot. Of course, the sheriff certainly thinks so now." She released an abrasive laugh.

"Too bad for you both. But as I told you in the diner, he's much too good for you…."

As Gretchen continued deriding Valerie for her shortcomings, a small crackling noise sounded in the distance. At first Valerie thought it was the fire, but then she heard it again—the muffled sound of footsteps. Or she could be imagining things. But then she saw it, a flash of white in the darkness, close to the ground and still several yards away. Help had arrived—to arrest them both. Fortunately Gretchen hadn't seemed to notice. Yet.

Valerie had to keep her distracted. Better still, she had to force her to confess. Whoever might be waiting in the shadows, she wanted them to know she had nothing to do with any of this.

Jabbing the shovel into the ground, she unearthed more dirt than she had before, thanks to a rush of adrenaline. "So tell me, Gretchen, how did you manage to plant that gun beneath my car?"

The woman had the audacity to look proud. "Oh, that was simple. About three weeks ago I waited until nightfall and while you were still cleaning up inside the diner, I found your car around back and stuck the gun right in the wheel well." Her grin was pure cunning. "I do so hate getting my hands dirty, so I wore gloves, which of course kept my fingerprints off the gun. Now, poking that hole underneath was a little more challenging, but I managed."

Valerie's mechanical problems had been the result of sabotage at the hands of a deranged killer. "You knew I would have to get it fixed and someone would find it."

"Precisely, although I didn't expect it to take quite that long. It's so hard to find good help these days, isn't it?"

Valerie shot her a fake look of understanding. "So true. And when you murdered Malcolm, how did you manage to get my hair planted on him?"

"I found that at the diner." She laid a slender hand on her throat. "You really shouldn't leave your hairbrush in a public restroom. It's a haven for DNA."

Valerie heard another rustle, and on the off chance it was Gavin, she began to whistle.

"You sound so happy, Valerie," Gretchen said. "Perhaps you're excited to finally see your grandmother's gold."

"I don't care about the gold," Valerie said. "I only want the diary and any documentation that's with the gold. You can take every last bit of it. By the time I walk back into town, you'll be well into Mexico."

Gretchen moved beside her and waved the diary. "Are you sure you really want this? It cost Jonathan Devlin his life."

Valerie halted the shovel. "You also killed Mr. Devlin?"

"Actually Malcolm Durmorr did, although he botched it the first time and sent the man into a coma. I had to persuade him to finish the job. One little injection into his IV and that was the end of that."

She spoke as if taking a man's life was a daily routine, sickening Valerie even more. "How exactly did you persuade Malcolm to do your dirty work for you?"

A devious smile curled her red-glossed lips. "Why, sex, of course. That's a powerful tool when it comes to men, but I suppose you already know that. How else would you have convinced Gavin O'Neal to take you into his home?"

Valerie clenched her jaw so tightly she thought her teeth might splinter. "Why did you kill Jonathan over Jess's diary?" she asked, although she suspected she already knew the answer.

"He's been blackmailing my family for years with it. However, I don't believe the whole story about my great-uncle Edgar stealing the gold and framing Jess. The Halifaxes have always been upstanding citizens. But the town would believe it, and my political aspirations would have been ruined."

"Considering Jake Thorne kicked your butt in the election, looks like you went to a lot of trouble for nothing." The minute Valerie muttered the words, she recognized her mistake when she saw the wrath in Gretchen's eyes.

"I believe we could use some more fuel for the fire." Gretchen held up the diary and waved it. "This might work."

Valerie rested her hands on the shovel's handle and assumed a relaxed posture that contrasted with her building anger. "Listen, you self-serving, sicko witch," she said in a remarkably even tone. "If you toss that into the fire, then you'll have to dig for the gold yourself."

"And I'll have to kill you now." That *now* part only confirmed what Valerie already knew—Gretchen intended to shoot her.

Gretchen surprisingly tossed the diary aside and, fast as a lightning bolt, grabbed the chain containing the pendant and yanked it from Valerie's neck, then hurled it into the darkness. "That's for the *sicko* comment. Now get back to work."

When Gretchen turned and picked up the diary, no doubt to toss it into the fire, Valerie saw her chance and took it. Bolstered by desperation, fueled by fury, she lifted the shovel and swung it with all the strength she could muster, landing it right between Gretchen's slender shoulders. The force of the blow sent the woman facedown in the dirt precariously close to the flames, her arms spanning outward and the gun spinning away.

Before Valerie could even move, Gavin was there standing over the prostrate Ms. Halifax, gun pointed at her head. "Don't move an inch, Gretchen, or I swear to God I'll kill you right now and save the taxpayers a lot of money."

"You'll pay for this," Gretchen muttered but failed to move. "You'll all pay."

Valerie decided that Gretchen's clichés indicated she spent way too much time watching old murder mysteries. But at least she hadn't gotten away with murder.

Suddenly a swarm of other men holding lanterns gathered around. Obviously the whole town. Obviously the whole county— maybe even several counties—had come in search of her.

"Good job, Valerie, making her eat dirt."

Valerie glanced past Gavin to Connor Thorne. "All in a day's work for Wonder Waitress," she said without any amusement in her tone.

With the adrenaline gone, Valerie collapsed onto the limb where Gretchen had been briefly seated a short time ago and rested her forehead on bent knees. Her mind whirled. Her head hurt—and so did her heart. Definitely her heart.

When she heard Gavin say, "Cuff her, Armstrong, and read her her rights," she lifted her head and held out her arms in front of her, wrists turned up. "I'm ready."

Gavin dropped down beside her, keeping a safe distance between them. "You're not under arrest. She is." He nodded toward a deputy guiding a handcuffed, raving Gretchen away into the darkness.

Valerie was glad that he finally believed her, yet hated that he hadn't all along. "You're not going to take me in, even for questioning?"

"No. I heard Gretchen's confession, all of it. And I don't know what to say to you other than I'm sorry."

Valerie was simply too weary to argue. "You were just doing your job." But that didn't change the fact he'd assumed the worst, like so many others in her life.

He took her hand in his. "Let's get you in the car so you can warm up."

Working her way from his hold, Valerie stood and tightened her jacket—his jacket—around her. "If I'm not under arrest, then I don't want to leave until I find what I've been searching for. You can have the gold. I only want answers."

He came to his feet. "Tomorrow. I'll personally see to it."

"I plan to leave tomorrow, so I want to do it tonight."

In his gaze she saw a flicker of sorrow that melted into resignation. "Okay. I'll start digging."

"I can do it."

Gavin caught her wrist and turned her palms up. "Your hands are raw. I'll take care of it. You sit by the fire and stay warm."

He grabbed the shovel from the ground and began to dig while Valerie sat by the waning fire feeling as if she might never be warm again. A few moments later, Connor came to his side and said, "I'll be glad to relieve you so you can see to Valerie."

Gavin handed him the shovel. "Thanks." He came back to her then and sat down, arms draped on bent knees as he stared off in the distance.

They remained that way for a time, silent, as if neither knew what to say or where to start.

"I should have let you talk last night," he finally said. "I knew something was seriously wrong. I just didn't want to hear it."

And she hadn't wanted him to hear it. "We can't change anything now, Gavin. It's done."

"But I should have known when I heard you say some things when you were sick. Things about not meaning to do it, that someone was hurting you." He leveled his gaze on her. "Who hurt you, Val?"

She'd had no idea he'd been privy to the fear that had come out in her dreams. "They were pretty rough when they arrested me. I remember the handcuffs biting into my wrists, the humiliation." She shuddered just thinking about it. "But I had a very nice, understanding judge who let me do community service at a shelter to work off my debt. That's why I decided I want to change my life and help others change theirs. I got a job waiting tables after that so I could work my way through college."

A slight smile curled the corners of his mouth. "That must be why you're so good at it."

"I've had a lot of experience." But not with anything like this. She'd never loved anyone this much and she'd never felt so helpless in her life, even when she'd had to worry over her grandmother's failing health and where the next meal would come from.

Another span of silence passed before the sound of approaching voices caught Valerie's attention. Several men emerged from the darkness holding shovels and lanterns and containers of coffee.

Gavin rose and greeted the first with a handshake. "Thanks for coming, Jake."

"Not a problem," the mayor said. "We've been in this together from the beginning. Might as well see it through now."

Jake took his place by Connor, his twin, at the site of the dig and they exchanged a few barbs not uncommon between brothers. Then Tom Devlin and even Logan Voss appeared—amazing since the man should be on a honeymoon or at the very least at home with his new wife.

Gavin turned and stared down on her. "We need to talk, but right now I need to help them so we can get this over with."

Valerie wasn't sure if he'd meant unearthing the treasure or ending their relationship once and for all. Whatever his intentions, she had no choice but to wait it out until they found the gold.

"Looks like you could use some of this."

She looked up to see Mark Hartman standing above her, holding out a cup of coffee, his brown skin bronzed by the glow of the fire. With his wide shoulders and solid build, he looked imposing, yet his smile was soft and sympathetic.

"Thanks," she told him as she accepted the coffee, grateful to have something warm to combat the cold, both outside and in.

He slipped his hands in his jacket pockets, looking decidedly uncomfortable. "Alli told me we were all wrong about you."

Dear, sweet Alli. "She's a very nice woman. You're lucky to have her."

"Yeah, she is. And if it's any consolation, Gavin never believed you were guilty. He argued with us about it. Guess we should have listened to him."

That was a great relief to Valerie, but she still wasn't sure if they could ever get past what had happened—his doubts, her deception. "It's okay, Mark. I understand why you would have thought the worst about me."

"But Gavin never really did," he insisted. "He loves you a lot. Just remember that." Following that comment, Mark grabbed a shovel and joined the others.

While the few remaining deputies stood back, together Gavin and his colleagues worked in sync, side by side, a band of broad-shouldered, honorable men, all members of the mysterious Texas Cattleman's Club.

Valerie marveled over their bond and wondered what it would be like to have such good friends. She'd had so few, had never known such camaraderie—until she'd met Gavin. He had been the best of friends, the best of lovers. She couldn't stand the thought that it might really be over between them, but she couldn't allow herself to hope, either.

"I've hit something," Mark said after a while. "Could be a rock."

Jake turned and signaled one of the deputies. "Bring a couple of lanterns over here."

Valerie bolted from the limb and stood behind the group while Gavin knelt by the man-made crater. "It's definitely not a rock," he said. "Keep going."

She held her breath as they continued to toss aside dirt at a breakneck speed.

"There it is," Logan said when the top of a brown leather trunk came into view.

After they lifted the chest from the ground and set it outside the fissure, Gavin turned to Valerie. "You should open it."

One of the deputies stepped forward, although he looked more boy than man. "Excuse me, sir, but should we disturb it since it's part of a crime scene?"

"It's hers, dammit!" Gavin hissed, causing the deputy to shrink back into the shadows. "Open it, Val."

As Gavin raised a lantern above her, Valerie crouched before the chest and lifted the rusting latch, holding her breath as she raised the lid.

Her gaze immediately snapped to Gavin. "It's empty."

"I'll be damned," Jake said. "Guess the gold was all a hoax after all."

Now Valerie would never have the answers she'd been searching for, and that made Gavin furious. All of this had been for nothing, all of her goals and dreams of piecing together her past. No good had come of it—except he had met her, a woman he would love for a lifetime. If she could forgive him.

Just to be sure nothing was hidden in the trunk, Gavin shone a flashlight into the interior and caught a glimpse of something in the corner. He knelt and retrieved a brown leather pouch and offered it to Val. "I think this is what you've been looking for."

Without speaking, she took the pouch and headed back to the fire, taking a seat on the branch. Gavin maintained his distance, like the rest of the men, while she opened it and withdrew some kind of document. Then she sat in silence for a few moments, scanning the text aided by a lantern—before she started to laugh.

Gavin immediately came to her side. "What's so damn funny?"

She rested a hand over her mouth, her blue eyes shining with tears. "They gave it all away."

Gavin frowned. "Who gave it away?"

"Jess and Brad. The sheriff she supposedly murdered. Brad Webster was my great-great-grandfather."

The guys gathered around and listened to Valerie explain how Brad had killed Edgar Halifax's men in defense of Jess. How they had returned years later, dug up the gold Halifax had stolen to frame Jess, had the marked bars melted into coins and then left them anonymously at orphanages all over the country. How they had married and changed their names before settling in St. Louis to build a new life, believing that the citizens of Royal would never have bought their story.

Valerie glanced up at Gavin before reading the last of the letter. "'I hope that whoever is reading this has learned a lesson from my experiences. Always remember, the real treasure in life is true love.'"

For a solid two minutes no one uttered a word. They all just stood there, toeing the ground and staring at the fire, until Connor said, "Guess everyone had Jess Golden pegged wrong. Just goes to show it's best not to jump to conclusions."

Gavin knew that all too well. His wrong conclusions might have cost him the best thing he'd ever had.

"Since we're obviously done here, let's all go home now," Jake said before patting Gavin on the back. "You two have a good night."

Gavin thanked them all one by one, then turned and offered his hand to Valerie. "We definitely need to go home."

Without taking his hand, Valerie stood. "My home's in St. Louis, Gavin, not here. Now that I know the truth, I can get on with my life."

Gavin hadn't experienced such pain since his parents' deaths.

He sure as hell had never felt so worthless. "You mean get on with your life without me."

She folded the letter and slipped it into her pocket without looking at him. "I can't spend my life with someone who doesn't believe in me, Gavin. And I can't expect you to forgive me for lying to you."

Dammit, he refused to let her go that easily. "You can't live with someone who loves you more than he's ever loved anything or anyone? Someone who does believe in you wholeheartedly even if he screwed up?"

She lifted her gaze to his. "You say this now, but what about later? What happens after everyone in Royal learns I'm the daughter of a murderer? That I have a criminal record myself? What then?"

"I don't give a damn what everyone thinks, Val." He heard the desperation in his voice and he didn't give a damn about that either. "I only care about you. And I'm willing to defend you for the rest of my life, if I have to."

She turned away from him toward the fire that was nothing more than a few embers. He walked up behind her and slipped his arms around her waist. "Look, people around here aren't as judgmental as you might think. They already accept you, and once they learn how you handled Gretchen all by yourself, you'll be a hero."

"I don't want to be a hero," she said quietly. "I just want…"

He turned her into his arms. "What do you want, sweetheart? I swear to God, I'll give it to you, whatever it is."

A stream of tears trailed down her cheeks. "I want you to love me for who I am. I don't want you to be ashamed of me or somewhere down the road decide you can never trust me. I want your respect."

"You don't get it, do you?" He thumbed a tear away from her chin. "I have never met anyone I respected more. You've shown me that I don't have to be a hard-ass to be a good sheriff. And God knows you've shown me what it feels like to love someone so much that it hurts." He tipped his forehead against hers and closed his eyes. "And if you leave now, I'll never open myself up again to anyone like I have with you. Never."

When she didn't respond, he knew she wasn't convinced. He knew he had lost her, probably for good.

Although it was by far the hardest thing he'd ever done, Gavin let her go and turned his back to her. "You can stay at the house tonight. I promise I won't say anything else or beg you or touch you. You can leave in the morning."

Skirting the hollowed-out spot that had once contained the legendary treasure, Gavin reached for the lantern resting below the tree and caught sight of the etchings—reminders of a love story that had gone right in spite of the odds. Even though it probably wouldn't matter, he withdrew his pocketknife and beneath the knothole, carved his initials, then Val's, divided by a heart.

Gavin rested his forehead against the trunk, one arm braced above, feeling as if he was about to lose it. He'd worked so long and so hard to protect his emotions, he'd actually convinced himself he couldn't cry. Then where the hell did the unexpected tears come from? Silent tears but no less real, no less painful. He didn't want her to know how badly he needed her, but some unknown force compelled him to take the knife again and begin to shape a jagged line—right down the middle of the heart he had carved.

Before he could finish, a hand came to rest on his shoulder. "Gavin, don't."

He pocketed the knife and swiped a forearm over his face. "That's pretty much how I'm feeling right now, Val. Like someone sliced my heart right open."

"I know."

He turned to her and saw her tears, but unlike him, she didn't bother to wipe them away. And with those tears went the last of his pride. "I can't stand the thought of you leaving me, Val. If you want me to beg you to stay, I swear I'll do it."

She released a ragged breath. "You don't have to beg. I'll stay."

Gavin had never heard more welcome words, had never experienced such undeniable relief. He tugged her to him, kissed her thoroughly and held her as if she might disappear. Reluctantly he pulled back and asked, "Are you sure?"

"I am now." She sighed. "I realize I was wrong not to trust you. But when I came here, no one knew where I'd come from, and I liked that. I could pretend to be just an average person and I didn't have to explain my past. I worried that if you knew about my mother and what I'd done, you wouldn't see me in the same way."

He pushed her hair away from her face and kissed her cheek. "Honestly I don't know how I would have felt if you'd told me in the beginning. After I got to know the real you, nothing you've done would have changed that. But I understand why you didn't trust me, and that's okay, as long as you trust me now."

"I do trust you, Gavin. And I love you with all of my heart." Her eyes went wide as her hand went to her throat. "Speaking of hearts, Gretchen tore off my pendant and threw it somewhere. I have to find it."

"I'll find it when I have some daylight. I promise you'll have your heart back."

She sent him a soft smile. "Probably not, because I've given it to you."

She definitely had his. "Then you'll stay here with me, no more talk of going back to St. Louis?"

"I need to go back for a few days. I have to say goodbye to several people. Actually kids I used to work with."

He was taking a chance, but he had to do it. "I want to go with you."

"I want you to go with me," she said, taking him by surprise. "I'd like the kids to meet you so they realize that not everyone in law enforcement is an enemy."

"I'd be glad to do it." And now for the ultimate question. "I want you to marry me, Val. We can do it after we come back— or before, if you want."

Indecision called out from her eyes. "We need some time, Gavin. We need the opportunity to get to know each other better before we take that step."

"But that's not exactly a no, right?" Hell, he sounded like a kid. An impatient one.

Her sudden smile eased Gavin's fear. "No, it's not a no. It's an 'I'll seriously consider it,' on one condition."

"What's that?"

Her smile expanded into a grin. "You stop sneaking up on me from behind."

He pulled her to him as close as he could, right against his heart that was fortunately still intact. "Is that in all cases or just when you're wielding something heavier than a feather duster?"

Her laughter echoed across the pasture. "Okay, maybe not all the time."

Gavin kissed the tip of her chilly nose. "Tell you what, I can't promise I'll never be behind you, but I do promise to warn you first. I don't want to end up kissing the ground, like Gretchen."

"And I promise not to smack you under any circumstance with anything more than my lips."

This time he laughed, but it died quickly when he looked into her eyes and saw concern there. "What's wrong?"

"We have a long way to go, you and me."

"As long as we go it together." He pushed her hair away from her face. "If you decide to see your mother somewhere down the road, I'll be with you every step of the way."

"I'll think about it," she said. "But in all honesty, I know she doesn't want to see me and I'm okay with that. Or I will be, as long as I have you."

She had him all right. And that's exactly where he wanted to be. "I'm not going to stop asking you to marry me until you say yes."

"And I'm not going to say yes until I'm good and ready."

"Stubborn woman," he grumbled.

"Persistent man."

"That's part of my charm."

She draped her arms around his neck. "And that's one of the many things I love about you."

"Good. Now let's go home and I'll show you just how charming I can be."

Gavin also planned to show her that a cynical sheriff, the once-confirmed bachelor, was capable of sharing his hardened heart, show her all of his love—and give her the gift of his trust.

Epilogue

From the diary of Valerie Raines-O'Neal

This is the newest volume of my journal and the beginning of my new life. Six months have come and gone since I found the answers to my past and the man who has changed my life. During that time, Gavin proposed to me at least once a week, sometimes twice, and told me he loved me every day. He even found my pendant that Gretchen so carelessly tossed away and added a heart with our names on it to start our own tradition—something to pass down to our children, along with our story.

Back in January we traveled to St. Louis together, where Gavin charmed all of the kids at the youth center. I said goodbye to my grandmother and I know that she's happy now that she's been reunited with her family, particularly Jess, who I'm sure had a hand in my happiness, too.

I wrote a letter to my mother, yet she never responded, and that's okay. I've forgiven her, the same as Gavin and

I have forgiven each other. I'm working on my master's thesis now, and in the meantime I've taken a job with the local children's bureau as a social worker. This allowed me to assist with Mark and Alli's adoption of Erika, which is now official. I've made good friends with Rose Windcroft Devlin, who now has a little girl she appropriately named Jessie—the baby who symbolizes the end of the feud between the Devlins and the Windcrofts. I also got to know the now-pregnant Melissa Voss while doing an interview, as well as Nita Windcroft-Thorne and Chrissie Thorne during various functions. I consider them good friends and their support has been invaluable. Oh, and Manny and Sheila, well, they have a brand-new set of twin girls. Serves Manny right.

I'm proud to say that Gretchen was convicted on all counts and is now serving several life sentences in a maximum-security women's correction facility on the other side of the state. I'm sure she finds the prison-issue clothing distasteful, and this gives me some satisfaction, although I'll someday forgive her, too, even if I never forget what she has done.

Last month I surprised Gavin by proposing to him. We married two weeks ago during the opening of the new memorial park on the grounds of my great-great-grandmother's former home. The Historical Society decided this was a fitting tribute to Jessamine Golden—the one-time outlaw and now honored citizen. The ceremony took place in the shadow of a beautiful bronze statue formed in the likenesses of Jess and Brad—another gift presented to me by Gavin. The service was simple, attended by a justice of the peace and witnessed by friends, including former and present members of the Texas Cattleman's Club—doctors, attorneys, law-enforcement agents, ranchers and firefighters and even Arabian royalty. I have never seen so many children and feel certain the members will contribute to populating Royal for many years to come, including my husband, who swears he'll have me pregnant by the end of the year. I'm not in any real hurry since I'm greatly enjoying the process.

I will never forget the look on Gavin's face during our wedding, the way he held my hands and the quiet reverence of his deep voice as he vowed to honor and love me all the days of his life. But the final words spoken will always remain etched in my heart—as they are also etched in the base of the statue. My great-great-grandmother's words of wisdom.

Always remember, the real treasure in life is true love.

I couldn't agree more, for when Gavin O'Neal entered my life, I became—and will always be—the richest woman on earth.

* * * * *

HARLEQUIN *Super Romance*

HOME TO LOVELESS COUNTY
Because Texas is where the heart is.

MORE TO TEXAS
THAN COWBOYS

by Roz Denny Fox

Greer Bell is returning to Texas for the first time since
she left as a pregnant teenager. She and her daughter
are determined to make a success of their new dude
ranch—and the last thing Greer needs is romance,
even with the handsome Reverend Noah Kelley.

On sale January 2006

Also look for the final book in this miniseries
The Prodigal Texan (#1326) by Lynnette Kent
in February 2006.

Available wherever Harlequin books are sold.

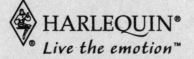

HARLEQUIN®
Live the emotion™

Silhouette Desire

COMING NEXT MONTH

#1699 BILLIONAIRE'S PROPOSITION—Leanne Banks
Battle for the Boardroom
He wants to control a dynasty. She just wants his baby. Who will outmaneuver whom?

#1700 ENGAGEMENT BETWEEN ENEMIES—
Kathie DeNosky
The Illegitimate Heirs
Sometimes the only way to gain the power you desire is to marry your enemy.

#1701 THE MAN MEANS BUSINESS—Annette Broadrick
Business was his only agenda, until his loyal assistant decided to make marriage hers!

#1702 THE SINS OF HIS PAST—Roxanne St. Claire
Did paying for his sins mean leaving the only woman he wanted…for a second time?

#1703 HOUSE CALLS—Michelle Celmer
Doctors do not make the best patients… Here's to seeing if they make the best bedmates….

#1704 THUNDERBOLT OVER TEXAS—Barbara Dunlop
She really wants a priceless piece of jewelry, but will she actually become a cowboy's bride to get it?

SDCNM1205